SINS OF VISCOUNT WORSLEY

Forever Yours Series

STACY REID

SINS OF VISCOUNT WORSLEY is a work of fiction. While reference might be made to actual historical events or existing locations, the names, characters, places, and incidents are either the product of the author's imagination or are used fictitiously, and any resemblance to actual persons, living or dead, business establishments, events, or locales are entirely coincidental.

First Edition September 2019

Edited by AuthorsDesigns
Copy-edited by Gina Fiserova
Proofread by Monique Daoust
Cover design and formatting by AuthorsDesigns
Stock art from Period Images

Dusean, always and forever.

JOIN MY NEWSLETTER

Sign up to be among the first to hear about my new releases, read excerpts you won't find anywhere else, and patriciate in subscriber's only giveaways and contest. I send out on dits once a month and on super special occasion I might send twice, and please know you can unsubscribe whenever we no longer zing.

Signup at: https://www.stacyreid.com/#newsletter

Happy reading!

Stacy Reid

PRAISE FOR NOVELS OF STACY REID

"**Duchess by Day, Mistress by Night** is a sensual romance with explosive chemistry between this hero and heroine!"—*Fresh Fiction Review*

"From the first page, Stacy Reid will captivate you! Smart, sensual, and stunning, you will not want to miss **Duchess by Day, Mistress by Night**!"—*USA Today bestselling author Christi Caldwell*

"I would recommend **The Duke's Shotgun Wedding** to anyone who enjoys passionate, fast-paced historical romance."—*Night Owl Reviews*

"**Accidentally Compromising the Duke**—Ms. Reid's story of loss, love, laughter and healing is all that I look for when reading romance and deserving of a 5-star review."—*Isha C., Hopeless Romantic*

"**Wicked in His Arms**—Once again Stacy Reid has left me spellbound by her beautifully spun story of romance between two wildly different people."—*Meghan L., LadywithaQuill.com*

"**Wicked in His Arms**—I truly adored this story and while it's very hard to quantify, this book has the hallmarks of the great historical romance novels I have read!"—*KiltsandSwords.com*

"One for the ladies...**Sins of a Duke** is nothing short of a romance lover's blessing!"—*WTF Are You Reading*

"**THE ROYAL CONQUEST** is raw, gritty and powerful, and yet, quite unexpectedly, it is also charming and endearing."—*The Romance Reviews*

OTHER BOOKS BY STACY

Series Boxsets

Forever Yours Series Bundle (Book 1-3)

Forever Yours Series Bundle (Book 4-6)

Forever Yours Series Bundle (Book 7-9)

The Amagarians: Book 1-3

The Kincaids series bundle (Books 1-3)

Sinful Wallflowers series

My Darling Duke

Her Wicked Marquess

Forever Yours series

The Marquess and I

The Duke and I

The Viscount and I

Misadventures with the Duke

When the Earl was Wicked

A Prince of my Own

Sophia and the Duke

The Sins of Viscount Worsley

An Unconventional Affair

Mischief and Mistletoe

A Rogue in the Making

The Kincaids

Taming Elijah

Tempting Bethany

Lawless: Noah Kincaid

Rebellious Desires series

Duchess by Day, Mistress by Night

The Earl in my Bed

Wedded by Scandal Series

Accidentally Compromising the Duke

Wicked in His Arms

How to Marry a Marquess

When the Earl Met His Match

Scandalous House of Calydon Series

The Duke's Shotgun Wedding

The Irresistible Miss Peppiwell

Sins of a Duke

The Royal Conquest

The Amagarians

Eternal Darkness

Eternal Flames

Eternal Damnation

Eternal Phoenyx

Single Titles

Letters to Emily

Wicked Deeds on a Winter Night

The Scandalous Diary of Lily Layton

CHAPTER 1

London, 1844
Mayfair, The Club

Michael Alexander St. Ives, Viscount Worsley, stared through the open windows of his private apartments at the young lady standing in the fog-shrouded street below his gambling club. She was handing out pamphlets, apparently desperate to save the lost souls who clambered up the steps into his particular brand of hell. Her efforts were a lost cause of course, as almost everyone sidestepped her or crumpled the sheet of paper and dropped it onto the cobbled streets. The sanctimonious moral prigs had yet to realize that people chose to enjoy life—or sinned as they called it—entirely of their own free will.

He couldn't quite place his finger on what about her had arrested his attention. The lady and her companion were not the first to protest his establishment in recent months, railing at his clientele to repent their ungodly ways. Perhaps it was her nervousness, evident to him though he glanced down at her from three stories above. It was the manner in which she kept stiffening at each carriage as they rattled up to the entrance of his lair. The way she lifted her shoulders before she walked with militant grace over to the gentlemen and carefully disguised ladies, handing them that small piece of paper which denounced him as the devil, leading the innocent men and women of London astray with the diabolical vices he offered in 'The Club.'

He drew deep on his cheroot, slowly releasing the smoke, studying her with an air of amused tolerance. She wore a dark blue dress and a matching hat with a narrow brim, her shoes were serviceable, and her gloves appeared well worn.

"Michael darling, I am not quite sure I understand your preoccupation with the streets below," Lady Temple said, from where she reposed with catlike grace on the sofa by the fire. A brief glance showed she had an affected pout on her thin lips. Her pale blue eyes narrowed in jealous contemplation, she snapped, "Is it that very odd creature who has snagged your regard? Upon my soul, it is quite alarming that you've been staring at her for several minutes now."

Lady Temple was always unhappy when attention shifted from her. She had been trying to entice Michael to her bed for almost two weeks. Nothing in him had stirred to play that particular seductive dance of cat and mouse. The lady saw him as a challenge and had boldly told him so, right before falling to her knees and reaching to unfasten the flap of his trousers. He had stepped away to her great annoyance, but she hadn't left, and for the moment he allowed her presence in his private rooms. Society would be thrilled and titillated with mock horror if they discovered he'd not taken a lover in eleven long months. Sometimes, that fact even astonished him whenever the awareness of his self-imposed celibacy jolted through him.

Eleven months.

The usual debauchery and scandalous pursuits of society seemed to no longer appeal to his jaded senses. Michael couldn't quite place his finger on when or why they had become less exciting and less satisfying to him. He was the purveyor of sin and vices, yet recently everything had become intolerably boring. His good friend, the Duke of Wycliffe, had suggested recently to him, that perhaps Michael really wanted a wife and children now and was ready to settle down to domesticity. He had stared at the duke, but only a feeling of icy horror had burned through his veins. The very idea of faithful monogamy terrified him.

"Good God, Wycliffe, it isn't a wife I hunger for. I am not like you who believe in that love claptrap."

"*What then?*" had been the duke's reply. "*And what is wrong in believing in love?*"

And Michael had had no answer, the void inside grew deeper, leaving him considerably puzzled as to the nature of his own malaise. It wasn't that he did not believe in love, he certainly saw enough people in society, giving each other ridiculously sappy smiles and sighs. He just hadn't felt the evidence of it for himself to feel any yearning for such affections. Nor did he perceive its benefits to make him desperately want love. He was not sure he would know how to recognize love if it came knocking on his door. With all the lovers he'd had over the years, he had never once felt the urge to look at one the way Wycliffe stared at his duchess. It was as if the damn man had lost all his senses. Nor had Michael ever given himself over to any vice—gambling, drinking, whoring, racing—he had too much awareness of self and control for that. Love seemed like a vice to his way of thinking. He had known men on the continent who fought duels in the name of love and had gotten themselves killed. Had known a few who cried into their liquor because of unrequited love, and those who even rashly spoke of killing themselves. *For love.* That could be the worst sort of vice in which a man could manage to get trapped.

He tore his gaze from the spectacle down below in the streets and stared at the countess. A bright, pleasing smile appeared on her mouth at finally securing his full attention. A gold-painted half-mask adorned her face, and her blonde hair was piled in a riot of curls above her slender neck. She lifted her chin, baring the delicate line of her throat to his gaze. Invitation glowed in her eyes, and her chest lifted rapidly as anticipation darkened her blue orbs.

"Vivian…" He lowered the glass of brandy he'd been nursing on the thick ledge of the windowsill. "I am not seeking a lover." How many times had he said that exact phrase in the last year?

She sauntered shamelessly close, pressing her body against his, yet nothing inside him moved.

"Neither am I. A night of glorious passion is what I am after. In the morning, I shall not care about you any further," she murmured with a wily smile.

"And won't your husband object to such an arrangement?"

She cast him an irritated glance. "I am certain he is now already abed with his *mistress*," she spat the words, pain, and anger shooting sparks from her eyes. "It is her alone he cares about."

"Ah…so is this revenge then? Are you to use me to make your earl jealous? And when you inform him that you've been bedded by the wicked Worsley and he challenges me to a duel and I kill him, then what?" he asked with chilling civility. "Is it widowhood you seek and believe I am the instrument of your brazen manipulation?"

She huffed and swirled away from him, slipping through the door heading back to the bowels of his club. Michael left his room and made his way down three flights of stairs and outside into the overly warm night air. He removed a matchbox from inside his coat and lit another cheroot. A few lords and ladies exchanged questioning glances at seeing him at the entrance to his club but nodded their heads in polite homage and continued inside.

He turned and stared at the force which had tugged him outside. It was quite astonishing, the way she captured his regard. Inexplicably, he lingered over her features. A slightly rounded face, elegant cheekbones, lush lips. He was too far away to discern her eye color, but it was evident she was a voluptuous woman of considerable beauty. She shifted, and her features were cast in the shadows, but she became aware of his regard for she had faltered into remarkable stillness. He stared openly, very willing to let her see his interest.

Michael was much used to the different religious groups protesting outside his gambling den shouting their moral hypocrisy and blaming him for the choices other men willingly made. Never had he seen a lady before, and he would not count that Quaker woman last month. She hadn't been a day under seventy with no reputation to lose. But this lady was young and sweetly curved in all the right places. The man who stood several feet from her clutched a bible along with his pamphlets. Perhaps her husband. Surely no young, unattached lady would be in London's dangerous streets at this hour, even if his club of ill repute was in the better half of town.

She was not unsettled by him in the least, lifting her chin, in a gesture of defiance.

Michael wanted to unsettle her. The idea surprised him into a laugh. He continued staring, trying to determine if he should approach her. But for what reason? Yet, Michael could feel his heart pounding faster, that dark and dangerous urge to coax and ravish sliding through his veins. What a paradox she presented, being so curvaceous and tantalizing, yet so demure and obviously out of his reach.

The awareness of that desire coursing through his veins felt like a punch in the gut. Despite earning the moniker of one of society's most profligate rakes, he had never taken a lover to his bed without much closer acquaintanceship. Certainly, his cock had never twitched from merely looking at a lady. With a scowl, he ruthlessly buried all traces of arousal, slowly calming the racing of his heart to its normal rhythm.

This unknown woman presented an unexpected appeal. And for the first time in months, Michael desperately wanted to indulge.

"*It* IS IN THERE, MARIANNE," Vicar Peter Ashbrook said, an expression of disgust carved into his face. "*That* is where she fell…and many others will too if we do not protest this disgusting attack on the moral fabric of our society. Those who sit in our pews are already saved. Jesus walked the earth to preach to sinners far and wide, and he was not afraid. So why should we be?" he demanded with righteous indignation, his dark green eyes so very much like her own filled with an agony of emotions.

"Yes, father," Marianne dutifully replied, clutching the

pamphlets her father had ordered printed in a tight grip, staring at the imposing stone building which housed it —*Sin*. That awful force to which her sister, Lucy, had fallen prey. The only information Lucy had revealed about her predicament was the gentleman she had fancied herself in love with had taken her in disguise to 'The Club,' and she had irrevocably lost all sense of herself.

This was the last place Marianne wanted to be when she should be home with her mother and sisters. But Papa had been determined to travel to London to find out what had happened to dear Lucy, and to bring the man who had ruined her to justice. Papa had been righteous in his fury and pain and had even packed a pistol in his luggage. Mama had wept with relief when Marianne had started packing too, refusing to let her father travel to town alone, especially when he did not seem at all rational.

The large dark red oak door opened, raucous laughter, revelry, and music spilled out into the air. Vices and wickedness were taking place within the dark recesses of that gambling den, where a man known to all and sundry as Lord Worsley—a viscount—owned and operated that sinful place. Marianne tried hard not to imagine the debauchery it enclosed. She had even heard he was vaunted for his profligacy and celebrated for it in some circles. And she suspected the man who had just exited that very door, *was* Viscount Worsley himself. Every part of her had been aware of him as he peered down from an open window like a dark angel. He stood under the weak beam of a gas lamp, yet the man seemed covered in darkness.

Her father handed her a few more pamphlets and headed toward the queue of carriages, not wanting any of the patrons heading into the club to escape a piece of his sermon.

Odd and terrifying sensations crashed against her

senses when the man unexpectedly sauntered in her direction. She glanced about, and no-one seemed interested in them, even her father was too preoccupied with the masked lady he was preventing from side-stepping him. He would want to save her, for he believed if only he had preached harder and been more vigilant, his daughter too might have been saved.

Marianne's thoughts scattered under a tide of confusion as the man stopped a few paces from her. He was devilishly handsome, and it was as if his mere presence stole the breath from her lungs. The man was tall with powerful shoulders, muscular legs, and appeared to cloak himself in a mask of civility and chilling elegance. He was clad in black from his longer than what was considered respectable hair to his feet, except for his snow-white shirt and cravat, and the deep burgundy silk waistcoat which fitted his lean frame to perfection. A straight nose and sharp, arrogant cheekbones lent an air of aristocratic breeding…and his eyes were the gray of tempered steel. *How beautiful.*

She was wicked, wanton at heart, to react so to a gentleman! Shame burned inside Marianne and she glanced away. Perhaps if she ignored his presence, he would not approach her. A shadow twisted with hers and she spun around. A harsh breath puffed from her to see him standing so close. "Sir! It is ungentlemanly of you to be this close."

"Ah…so you are a lady who still has expectations of polite conduct even though you are hovering outside of a den of ill repute?"

She flushed at the amusement which leaped into his eyes. Selecting one of the pamphlets she handed it to him. "If I could leave this with you, Sir, I am certain it may help when you need it."

A brow arched and he perused the piece of paper, slanting it towards the beam of the lamp. "It seems that I prey on the weak and those addicted to gambling to ruin their souls. It also seems that I ruin good men and women for my own evil gain." He slanted her a probing glance. "And do you really believe this?"

"That you lead good men and women astray?" She only had to think about her sister and arrive at the truth. "Yes, I do, and without any conscience."

"And do you not believe some vice to be tolerable and needed by men and women of society?" the dark angel asked, a crooked yet so attractive smile slanting his lips, "as a sort of release from the tedium of life?"

Marianne's heart jerked, and she felt mortified for having even noticed his handsomeness. She cast a quick glance at her father, who was too busy handing out his pamphlets and warning away a potential customer of the wickedness to be found in those gambling walls and why they should stay away.

"No…any sort of indulgence would only lead to further decay," she said stiffly.

"I provide employment to young ladies whose only other alternative would be to walk the streets of London. Surely there is honor in that?"

Oh, why did she feel as if he mocked her?

"I am certain you could offer more honorable work!"

"My business is not in the red-light district," he refuted smoothly. "There you will find numerous whorehouses and more profligate gambling dens…should you not take your righteous protests there instead?"

A flush went through her body, and his eyes sharpened. Suddenly Marianne felt like a field mouse under the piercing stare of a hunting hawk. Interest lit in his eyes, his expression shifted ever so slightly, and she felt as if the devil had come knocking at her door.

"Ah…a true innocent, and how prettily you blush," he drawled with wicked provocation.

Before she could blink, he had taken hold of her and tugged her into a dark pocket of shadows, where the light from the gas lamp did not reach them at all. Even the fog seemed to be directed by his will, as it curled around them, shrouding them more into dark obscurity.

He lifted one hand and lightly cupped her cheek. Shock scattered her thoughts, and her hands flew up in automatic defense to rest on a solid wall of warmth and vitality. A tremor ran through her at the feel of his thumb so close to her lips. "Si…Sir!"

"It has been a long time since I've had the urge to kiss a woman," he murmured darkly.

Her heart jerked, but she stood still, trying to understand the weakness assailing her. "I'll scream," she murmured huskily. "And my father has a pistol."

"Concerned about me?"

"No."

That crooked smile appeared again. "I wouldn't have pounced; I was about to ask permission to kiss you."

She sucked in a sharp breath. As if she would allow her first kiss to be with such a wicked rogue. "Denied."

He lowered his arm. "Pity. It would have been delightful."

"For you, perhaps! Men like you only use and discard."

His head canted left. "Men like me?"

"Rakes and seducers of innocents, who take what they want without any thoughts or consequences for the ladies they leave behind!"

"I would have only left you after I've wrung every

scream, and moan of pleasure from your lips, and release from your body. You would be satisfied, I promise."

Marianne's hand flew as if it had a life of its own to slap his cheek, but he caught her hand in a gentle clasp. The wretched man pressed a kiss to her gloved knuckles, and she felt the heat of his lips through the material.

"There are only wolves in these parts of town, you should stay away, my lady."

Then he stepped back, whirled around, and made his way back inside his club.

"Marianne?" her Papa shouted, spinning around.

One step forward and she left the pocket of darkness. Relief lit in his eyes when he saw her. "Our work here is done. I promised your mother we would come home for the weekend, and we must keep that promise."

She nodded, relief worming through her. "Yes, Papa." And they made their way down the darkened streets. As her father hailed a hackney, Marianne couldn't help glancing behind her once more.

CHAPTER 2

Wiltshire,
Three weeks later…

Miss Lucy Ashbrook's child was on the way.

A tight tension had gripped the occupants of the charming five-bedroom cottage, situated in the heart of Biddleton as they awaited the birth. There was no jubilant expectation, only a feeling of severe anxiety and fear. Mamma had often remarked that her husband's staunch sense of moral propriety was fashioned from their queen. He was so very proper, their father, and how it had shamed him that Lucy had fallen with a child out of wedlock. Since Mama had made the discovery of Lucy's swollen belly, Papa had not been able to bring himself to speak with her. And Lucy cried almost daily, begging for his forgiveness only to be met with a countenance of harsh rigidness. Lucy, at nineteen and the third eldest daughter, might have been honorably married if not for her waywardness and the vile actions of her dishonorable seducer.

Lucy's screams tore through the chilly night air,

piercing, and pain-filled. For the third time in the last hour, the youngest Ashbrook sister, Sarah, promised she would never follow the path of shame and disgrace her sister had followed.

"I'll be a good girl, Mama," she said while sending fretful glances upstairs where Lucy labored to bring her bastard child into the world with only their mother and servants attending her.

A few minutes passed, and then another scream from Lucy echoed through the cottage, followed by a thin wail.

"The baby is here!" Sarah cried, gripping the edges of her skirts, and taking the stairs two steps at a time.

Over an hour had passed since the baby's arrival, and Marianne had stayed in the parlor, knitting a blanket which she had been working on for the last few days. Mrs. Evans who served as their housekeeper and cook bustled in with a tray with tea and cakes and lowered it on the walnut table.

"Thank you, Mrs. Evans," Marianne murmured, lowering her knitting needles.

"Lucy will be quite all right, Miss Marianne," she said with a kind smile.

Marianne nodded, poured a cup of tea from the round china pot, and took a sip. Warmth flooded her body, and some of the tension which had invaded her limbs eased. Setting the cup on the table, she stood, walked over to the window and parted the curtains which had seen better days, a lump forming in her throat. Papa paced around the small garden he tended with such diligent care, a harsh frown splitting his brow. He had been outside for a few hours, ever since Lucy had gone into labor.

Out of his six daughters, one had already wretchedly fallen, and the people in their small village of Biddleton held their collective breath for the other Ashbrook girls to follow suit. Marianne thought it ridiculous for the reasons they had been labeled as 'fallen' to her mind could be called misadventures and be forgiven quite easily. But it seemed there was an even stricter code of conduct for the vicar of the parish's daughters.

As it stood, no-one outside of the family and their three servants were aware of Lucy's enceinte state. Mrs. Evans, Beatrice—the scullery maid—and Agatha the maid who attended her mother and the older girls had all been sworn to secrecy by their father. If the people of Biddleton should discover Lucy's situation, Papa might perhaps lose the faith and confidence of his parishioners, and even Countess Huntley who had allowed him the living might be displeased enough to remove herself as Papa's benefactress. He could not afford to lose his living in Biddleton.

Still, Marianne could not bear to support her father's plan of sending Lucy's child to an orphanage. Footsteps clambered down the stairs, and Mama entered the parlor with her girls behind her. She smiled, and there was joy in that smile, even if she appeared tired. Mamma tucked a wisp of raven black hair behind her ears.

"It is a girl," she said softly, her brown eyes dark with worry. "A most beautiful...perfect child. Oh, Marianne..." she closed her eyes briefly, seemingly struggling to contain her emotions.

"Another girl?" she asked with a smile, lacing her fingers tightly together lest they trembled.

As Mama told the story with each of her pregnancies, their father had prayed for a son, and each time he had been blessed with another daughter. He'd often told them the good Lord must have known what he was doing to gift him with such wonderful girls.

A lump formed in Marianne's throat, and her mother

pressed a hand over her lips, her eyes were red from fighting back the tears.

"Agatha has helped me bathe Lucy, and she is resting."

"Should we tell Papa?" Ruth asked, looking at the worn carpet instead of her family.

Marianne looked through the windows of their small cottage at her father, pacing in the garden once more. He lifted his face to the sky for several moments, and then his shoulders relaxed. She tightened her fingers on the curtains until they ached. That meant he had reached a decision. He walked with purpose toward the front door, and when she heard it slam, she released the curtain and turned to greet his arrival into their small but very tidy parlor.

Their father entered, a still very handsome man of only eight and forty, with only a dash of gray in his hair. His face was unwrinkled over time, and he boasted a lean and fit body from his long walks which he took daily. He had also been active in helping a few farmers and miners with whatever they were struggling to repair, whenever they needed the assistance. Her father was a good man, and it pained Marianne to see him struggle with Lucy's fall of grace.

Their mother released Sarah and clasped her hands before her. "Have you decided, Husband?"

He glanced at his girls present—Marianne, Sarah, Ruth, and Maggie—and nodded once.

"I've asked God about it and gave my worries to Him. We will take the child to one of the orphanages in Bethnal Green and never speak of this again."

Her mother paled but did not refute his edict. Ruth started to cry silently, and she gripped Sarah's and Maggie's hands.

Marianne stepped forward. "Papa! This baby will be your grandchild...and my niece! How could you bear the idea of sending her away to an orphanage to live an indifferent life that might be filled with pain and hardship?"

"Marianne," he began wearily. "This is the best decision for the family—"

"You mean the best decision for you!"

"For the family!" he roared, his eyes darkening with ire. "Do you know the hardship you girls would face if it became known your sister had acted the whore and has given birth to a bastard?"

She flinched and stumbled back. "Lucy is not a wh… whore, Papa," Marianne choked out. "She made a foolish, foolish mistake. Please, if—"

"No," he said in that voice that allowed no room for other possibilities. "No-one in Biddleton knows of our shame, and we will keep it that way, or we will lose our reputations and possibly my livelihood. All respectable paths would be closed to this family because of your wretched sister. If we keep that child, we risk greater ruin and disgrace!"

Their mother stood and smoothed nonexistent wrinkles from her gown. Her eyes glowed with pain and tired acceptance. To Marianne's mind, her mother, who even at three and forty was a great beauty with no gray hair or wrinkles, appeared to have aged. Mamma swallowed and lifted her chin. "I'll go up and speak to Lucy and—"

"May I do it, Mama?" Marianne asked, wiping at the tears trailing down her cheeks.

Her mother knew of the guilt Marianne carried with her each day. She was the eldest sister at three and twenty, and she had failed her sister. Lucy had been in London to experience its beauty at the invitation of their aunt. Marianne had known there was someone Lucy fancied being in love with, and that he was 'wealthy and dashing and terribly handsome.'

She had seen the path to ruin and had warned her sister most severely, but Marianne hadn't informed her mother and father of her misgivings so that their father could demand Lucy's return from London. Instead, Marianne had trusted that Lucy would have listened… rather, she had returned home six months' ago with a babe in her belly and no word on whom had gotten her into this mess and abandoned her.

"Yes," her Mama said with a soft smile of approval.

She faced her father. "May I inform her of your decision tomorrow, Papa?"

"No."

"Papa! Lucy will not sleep if—"

"We've had no rest in this house since we learned of her deceit and wanton heart! She will know of the heartache her family has endured," he snapped, before storming from the small parlor to his study.

Marianne could not bear looking at her sisters and mother, so she whirled about and went up the stairs to Lucy's room. Marianne entered without knocking, not wanting to disturb her niece if she slept. A fire burned in the grate, and a tired Lucy lay upon her side, peering at a swaddled pink bundle resting next to her, an expression of awe and profound love on her face.

Lucy glanced up when she entered. "Oh, Marianne," she whispered with a tremulous smile. "She is so very beautiful. I would like to call her Elizabeth—Lizzie seems more appropriate until she is of age."

Marianne sat on the edge of the bed. "Lizzie, it is a beautiful name."

Lucy pressed a finger to the baby's forehead.

"I still cannot believe she is real," she said, her voice thick with emotions. "and so beautiful and perfect…"

Marianne hadn't the heart to refute her claims of perfection when all she saw was a pink bundle with wrinkled skin. It felt cruel to inform Lucy now of their father's decision, but he would climb those steps and do it himself and in a far crueler manner. The very idea was unbearable.

"What happened, Lucy?" she questioned softly. "How…who is the father? I have asked you several times since you've returned home, and you have remained tightlipped. That has to stop now."

Lucy did not meet her eyes, but a flush ran from her face down to her neckline. "That is not important now. All that matters to me is Lizzie and protecting her. As soon as I am strong enough, I shall find respectable employment. I heard that Squire Dawson is seeking a governess for his girls. He had always been kind to our family. I am certain he will consider my application."

Marianne's heart broke into dozens of pieces. "Papa… Papa said she cannot stay, Lucy. He will not pretend that you were married…and your husband died on the trip home."

Her sister's gaze collided with hers, and horror filled Lucy's eyes. She struggled to sit up fully, and Marianne rushed to help prop the pillows behind her.

"Please, Marianne," she cried, "what did Papa say?"

As succinctly as possible, she informed her sister of their father's decision. Lucy paled, her throat worked, and then a raw, ugly sob burst from her before she contained it. "An orphanage?" she whispered weakly. "And we might never know her?"

"Yes."

They stared at each other, the pain of that decision

heavy in the room. Lucy closed her eyes, torment etched on her face. "I am so foolish, he promised…he *promised* me we would marry, and our family would be well."

She reached out and clasped one of her sister's hands between hers. "Who, Lucy? If you were to name him, Papa could go to him, and there might be a different outcome."

Her sister swiped at the tears coursing down her face. "He told me he loved me," she cried piteously.

Lucy's pain pierced somewhere deep inside Marianne, filling her with anger. "Who is he!"

Her lips flattened in a stubborn line. "He'll not marry me, and Papa does not have the connections to force his hand."

"Yes, Lucy, but there might be a chance he'll take his child, and she might be saved from the cruelty of an orphanage."

Lucy froze, hope filling her expression. "I…do you think so?"

"If there is such a chance, we must take it. Will you… will you please tell me who this man is?"

"Only if you promise me to take Lizzie to him yourself, along with a let…letter from me."

"Oh, Lucy," Marianne said, releasing her hand. "It would be Papa who would go, and he would not take any letter to this man who has ruined you so shamelessly."

"You know Papa would do something foolish like attempting to challenge him to a duel, which is highly illegal, and Papa would be in trouble. This man is wealthy and powerful, if he wishes it, he could ruin Papa in one crushing blow. Please, Marianne, you *must* go."

Unease flared through Marianne. "How powerful?"

Lucy looked away briefly. "He is a lord."

"A lord!"

She looked embarrassed and confused and regretful. "Yes."

A hollow sensation invaded her midsection. "Oh Lucy, and you *believed* such a man would marry you? Lords marry young ladies with dowries, unsullied reputation, and connections," she said, staring at her foolish sister. "How could you have fallen for the words of a seasoned rake!"

Lucy dropped her head against the pillow and stared at the ceiling. "Oh Marianne, I have been asking myself that very same thing since I discovered my situation. He was so very amiable and good-natured, and so handsome and charming. He paid me such attention, but now that I look back at it, there was no public or open courting. Everything had a secretive air about it. Yet I believed him then when he promised how much he loved me and wanted to be with me always."

A dark feeling swelled through her. That wretched liar! She wished she could take Papa's pistol, find him and place a bullet in his wicked heart. How she wished she could defend Lucy's honor. "You are equally to blame for this situation," Marianne said. Lucy had been well aware of the impropriety of her conduct, having been carefully instructed in the rules governing the social conduct of young ladies by their mother and governess.

"Marianne—"

"No, you are, Lucy. You knew better, but you allowed passion to cloud your good senses. Did you inform him of your state?"

"Yes," she said through bloodless lips. "I did."

"And he refused to marry you still," Marianne said, tears forming in her eyes, imagining how much heartbreak and pain her sister must have endured at that moment.

"He might do the same thing father wants to do. Place

Lizzie in an orphanage. That is what lords do with their unwanted bastards," Lucy said with a touch of bitterness.

A heaviness lodged in Marianne's stomach. "I have to try. Perhaps he might feel different about a child, especially if he has any of the goodness you saw."

Even to her ears, that hope felt empty. What good man would abandon a girl he had compromised? "Perhaps I will be able to convince him of his duty and responsibility to this child." *And to you.* "I might be able to convince him to settle Lizzie with an inheritance, so her future is not so bleak, or to provide you with a living where you could go far away from here with her, and live comfortably with a servant or two, and assume widowhood as you wanted."

A painful hope lit in Lucy's face. "Oh Marianne, that would be more than I ever dreamed."

"If you have that financial independence, we might be able to convince Papa to let you go. I am to travel to town in a few weeks to interview for that governess's post with Lord Sanderson. I will convince Papa it should be me and Mama who takes Lizzie to the orphanage…and then I will plead with Mama to allow me to take her to London."

There was a long pause, while her sister seemed to agonize over what to do.

"And do you think Mama would do that…for me?"

She squeezed Lucy's fingers. "Mama does not want Lizzie in a poorhouse either. Surely, she will see that I should take her to her father than to be left at a place where she might suffer."

"Lord Worsley," Lucy finally whispered.

A jerk of shock pierced Marianne, and memory of that dark angel and his touch against her face rose to the surface. "*What?*"

Haunted eyes lifted to Marianne's, and a breath

shuddered from Lucy. "The man I loved…the man who ruined me is Lord Worsley."

The most awful sensation of panic coiled around Marianne's lungs, tightening until she could not breathe. Could such a man be convinced to do anything he did not want to do?

Dear God.

CHAPTER 3

4 months later…
Russell Square, London.

There was a loud and very off-putting commotion in Michael's hallway.

"You, madam, will leave this house at once!"

His normally unflappable butler—Carlton—had raised his voice, enough so that it filtered in the drawing-room several doors down. The lady must have made some reply. However, Michael did not hear it. Somehow, she retained her calm in the face of his butler's stern demeanor.

"It is no concern of yours where my master is," Carlton replied in that stiff upper lip way of his. "My lord is not at home to any callers today, and most certainly not to…to someone disgraceful enough to barge inside uninvited!"

The interest that had been absent for the last few minutes slithered through him. Michael slowly lowered the brandy to a small desk before the chaise longue in which he sat and sent the very naked widow Benchley a small smile.

"If you will excuse me for a moment, my dear. I shall return shortly."

She pouted, before draping herself over the chaise, taking up his drink and placing the glass to where his lips had just been. Her lids fluttered closed on an exaggerated groan, and he bit back his smile and made his way from the drawing-room.

"I shall not leave until I've seen Viscount Worsley and if you try to touch me again, Sir, I'll not hesitate to slap you with this umbrella!"

A smile tugged at his lips as he moved silently toward the tableau.

"He is not in residence," his butler said.

"He *is*, and I know this because I followed him. Then I paid the driver of my hired carriage to wait fifteen minutes while I worked up my courage to come and knock on this door. I am tired and dusty from traveling, and you Sir, will show some kindness and summon your master!"

Even more interesting. Michael could not recall if he'd ever had a lady do that before. At his approach, the young lady spun around. An unfamiliar, heavy feeling constricted his chest. "I know you," he murmured, staring at her eyes. "Ah, they are an exquisite green of new spring leaves."

The color rising on her cheeks riveted him. She had such an enchantingly pretty face, with a lovely, lush mouth, and a most determined chin. Unexpectedly he felt lighter as if her mere presence had brightened his day somehow.

"If I might have a moment of your time, my lord, it is very urgent." She gripped the handle of the basket she carried, a basket which appeared to have something covered up. A puppy, perhaps. It did not escape him that somehow, she had dragged in two valises and a hatbox along with the basket. How…odd.

"If you will follow me." He glanced at Carlton. "Have Mrs. Barrett arrange for tea, cakes, and some sandwiches to be sent to the smaller drawing-room."

Relief lit in the lady's gaze, and he wasn't mistaken there was a sheen of tears. The blanket over the basket moved again, and then a soft cry lifted from it.

The very air around them went remarkably still. She stared at him, rather pale at first, and then flushing, and turning away her face. With surprising deftness and strength, she lifted the basket higher and shifted the soft blanket to reveal a rounded cherubic face with a tuft of blonde hair. The face which had been creased in a cry smoothed out, and the baby cooed instead.

"And who is this?" he asked with lethal softness, a disquiet to her presence piercing him.

Her gaze volleyed from him to his butler, and a violet blush painted her cheeks. She lifted her chin. "If we could have some privacy, my lord, I shall explain all."

He spun and made his way to the smaller drawing-room, and she hurried behind him. Once at the door, he held it open and allowed her to precede him inside. He closed the door firmly, and moving to the sideboard, he grabbed a decanter and poured a generous splash of brandy into a glass. He swallowed down the liquor, the smooth burn welcoming before he faced her. Something told him he needed the fortification.

"Why have you called at my home with this child?" he demanded bluntly.

She placed the basket on the chaise longue and seemed to do a quick check over the child's body. What she looked for was beyond Michael's comprehension. Seemingly satisfied, she laced her fingers together and met his gaze unflinchingly. Except, he could see the wild flutter of her pulse at the base of her throat. The lady was quite frightened and doing her best to appear unflappable.

"Surely you must suspect," she said, casting a glance at the basket.

"I assure you, I haven't the remotest guess."

"I'm Miss Marianne Ashbrook, sister of Lucy."

She waited as if that introduction would explain her presence in his home. He merely arched a brow, and that was enough to prompt her to further speech.

"I have taken a considerable risk to come here, my lord."

"Did you?"

"Yes, I lied to my father and journeyed for several days alone from Wiltshire. Papa believes I've taken up a governess's post somewhere in London, not that…not that I am *here*."

"And that considerable risk is a lie?" he asked with biting sarcasm.

"Of course, it is." She sniffed delicately. "I expect a man of your wicked principles to think a lie to one's parent negligible. Oh, forgive my loose tongue, your lordship, I am not here today to scold you for your wicked ways, but for a far more important matter."

Something softened unexpectedly inside Michael. "On the contrary, I find honesty refreshing and important in any relationship. Your reminder is appreciated, Miss Ashbrook. I must disappoint you, however, as I am not familiar with Lucy."

She stiffened, and the pain radiating from her gaze had him lowering his drink to the walnut table and taking a few steps closer. "Miss Ashbrook—"

"You do not remember her?" she asked so softly it was a wonder he heard.

There was a strong possibility he had met this Lucy and forgotten her. Each week he met dozens of ladies at balls, routs, and soirées, and dozens of more lush ladies at his gambling den. He saw that she was looking bewildered and said with some impatience, "Why is it important that I know her?"

"I…" she took a steady breath, a beguiling pink blossoming over her face and throat. "Lucy fell with child after spending some time with you, Lord Worsley. I've brought your child to you."

Michael stared at her for several moments, unable to credit her accusation.

"*My* child?" he asked, unable to keep an inflection of surprise out of his voice.

"Yes, your child. I am very much shocked by the whole affair."

"Are you the mother?"

"Please pay attention, your lordship, Lucy is the child's mother," she said, not mincing words.

He glanced at the basket where the child laid seemingly content with the world if the soft gurgles were anything to go by. A child…and it was supposed to be his.

"How old is the child," he asked softly.

"Four months old yesterday."

The knot in his gut loosened, and a slow exhale puffed from him. "Then, the child is not mine."

"I beg your pardon!"

"I haven't had a lover in a long time."

"And what does that have to do with anything?" she demanded, her tone mildly reproving.

"Don't be a pea-goose," he snapped, low and hard. "The timeline of this bundle of joy suggests I can't be the father. Also, I have always taken care *never* to leave my seed in a lover!"

She swayed at his explicitness, pressing a gloved hand to her cheek. Miss Ashbrook appeared very much flushed, and with tears sparkling on the ends of her long eyelashes. "I…my sister would not lie to me, not about something this important."

It galled him unspeakably that her tone suggested he was the liar in the situation. "Whatever fraudulent—"

"There is no fraud here, your lordship," she cried with passionate alarm. "If you would but *look* at her. Her eyes are the same as yours…the beauty of ashen clouds chasing a storm."

Her earnestness rocked him back on his heels, and for precious moments he could only stare at Miss Ashbrook. Michael went over to the child, and as he peered down at her, an inexplicable feeling blossomed through him. He could not identify it, never having endured such a sensation before. If he were a different type of man, perhaps he would label it as awe with a dash of fright. He didn't believe he had ever been this close to a child before. He examined her plump and clean features. Her eyes were indeed a silver-gray, and her hair was a shade lighter than his dark blond. He moved the blanket aside, his heart pounded and lifted one of the tiny baby's arms.

There it was, the red crescent-shaped birthmark that seemed to be on every St. Ives. "And your sister named me to be the father?" he demanded gruffly.

"Yes," she said on a tremulous sigh. "Our father…" she cleared her throat. "To protect the family's reputation, our father wished to send Lizzie to an orphanage in Bethnal Green. Our Lizzie cannot go there! We…Lucy and I were hoping you would claim her and provide a loving home for her. With you, surely her life would be better and her future brighter."

He heard the desperate, agonizing hope in Miss

Ashbrook's tone. Either through a misunderstanding or some mishap, Lucy Ashbrook contrived to say they had been lovers.

Except…this child was not his. He suspected his bounder of a brother, Thomas St. Ives, the heir apparent to the viscounty.

"Before you make a decision, I believe you should read this."

She dipped into the pocket of her dress and withdrew a letter. He took it, noted there was no wafer, and unfolded the piece of paper.

Dearest Thomas,

I waited for you by our bench in Hyde Park as I promised, and you never showed. I came back for several days, with such hope in my heart that you would be there. I did not see you at any balls in the week to follow, and I cannot express how much my heart shattered. I loved you sincerely, and I believed you held me deep in your affections as well.

I want to say I forgive you for leaving me alone after you promised to marry me. I cannot. But I feel you owe your daughter everything, even if she was born out of wedlock, she was conceived in love. I cannot bear for her to be sent away to a home. It devastates me that she is being taken away from me, but my heart might heal if I know she is being cared for by you and not indifferent strangers who will be more interested in the money they receive for her instead of her well-being.

Lucy.

A vague memory resurfaced in his thoughts, and he clenched his teeth to bite back his snarl of anger.

"*I want your blessing to marry Lucy Ashbrook. She is the most perfect angel I've ever seen. Sweet and charming, and so very pleasant.*"

Thomas had been drunk at the time, and Michael hadn't taken his brother seriously. And now he had a bastard in the world, and a young lady was ruined. Thomas was currently affianced to Lady Sarah Balfour, the Earl of Kenwood's daughter. His brother would consign the child to an orphanage so as not to embarrass his fiancée and powerful father-in-law should this scandal reach the ears of the gossipmongers of society.

Michael did not think to protest his innocence in this matter again. To do so would require him to cast the blame on his brother. It would be best if all eventual scandal were directed at Michael. Society already referred to him as the wicked viscount and expected this sort of behavior from a man of his reputation. He knew Thomas to be a brilliant young man who had graduated Cambridge with honors. How he had come to abandon a pregnant Lucy was beyond Michael. Surely his objections to his brother's marriage to a girl with no dowry and connections hadn't been all it took from Thomas to move on?

Many orphanages were really a place where unwanted babies were dumped for a penny here or there. Not many lived beyond a few weeks for the living conditions were cold and harsh.

What a bloody mess.

"Very well, you may leave the child here," he said abruptly.

Michael needed time to determine his next steps and what it would mean that he now had a child, the very last thing he ever expected, in his life to care for. He scrubbed a hand over his face.

What a damn complicated mess.

"I BEG YOUR PARDON?" Marianne asked faintly, pressing a hand to her chest.

The viscount stared at her with an unfathomable expression. She had come prepared with so many arguments in the desperate hope he would show some kindness. His capitulation was unexpected, and that he did so without any bluster rattled her nerves.

His expression was grim as he pinned her with his stare. "You may leave the child, Miss Ashbrook. Thank you for bringing her to me."

She waited for relief to fill her bones, but only a deep disquiet filled her veins. And anger. That he would so easily discard thoughts of Lucy. He had not even thought to ask after the young girl he had ruined and cast to the scrutiny and condemnation of society. How silly of her to even expect a glimmer of remorse from an unprincipled seducer.

She tried to gather her scattered thoughts. "And what of Lucy?"

He sustained this query with no more than a blink "And what of her?"

"She is ruined."

He was perfectly silent for a moment, a tiny crease between his brows. "By her own desires. It takes two to make a child, Miss Ashbrook, surely even with your *naïveté* that is general knowledge."

She flushed. "She was callously seduced—"

"Ah…that old belief that a man only has to kiss a lady and she becomes enraptured, loses all of her senses, and is quite blameless in the game of seduction. I assure you, *that* is not the way of it. Your sister was equally complicit and very well knew what she was about when she allowed herself to be ravished."

"My sister was a girl of eighteen years and you a man of the world! Above everything, you are shameless! Surely you can see that you took advantage and must make some restitution."

"I will do my best to make amends, but it will not be marriage. It is too late for that."

She squared her shoulders and lifted her chin, but her lips trembled fiercely as she battled the fierce urge to cry. "I see."

"I'll purchase a house in the countryside and will write a draft for five thousand pounds for your sister in the hopes it will at least provide a comfortable future."

Marianne stared at him in ill-concealed shock. "That is a fortune," she whispered in a stupefied tone. It was more than she expected, yet the fact he showed such little care for Lucy hurt somewhere deep inside. "Lucy has not yet reached her majority. I am not certain Papa will allow her to keep that money."

Papa had already cuttingly referred to Lucy as a whore, Marianne wasn't entirely sure he would see this as restoration toward securing Lucy's future. "It might be best if it goes toward Lizzie's dowry and her education."

"The child's dowry will be much more than five thousand pounds, and her education will be provided by the best governesses and tutors."

He appeared honest, sincere, and she was at a loss for words.

The viscount continued, "I will speak to your father as soon as it is feasible."

"My father will likely shoot you," she said with blunt honesty. "He is very angry and hurt about the entire affair."

"I will navigate those waters when the time comes," he said enigmatically.

There did not seem to be anything to say in reply to this. She glanced toward the basket. "Lizzie will need a wet nurse immediately, someone who loves children and has a good temper. A room will need to be converted—"

The connecting door to the larger drawing-room opened, and a lady, if Marianne could call her that, framed the doorway, draped in a sheer peignoir. A mass of brown hair with streaks of red tumbled to the lady's back in loose waves, her eyes had a limpid cast, and to Marianne's utter shock, she could see the lady's breasts through the sheer material. Even on the floor behind the lady, there were scattered unmentionables on the ground, and her gown, gloves, and hat were also discarded on the chaise longue. She shifted her gaze to the viscount. Good heavens, she had interrupted a *tryst*!

"Darling," the unknown lady drawled provocatively, tousling her hair. "How much longer must I wait?"

Marianne glared at her. How unspeakably outrageous!

CHAPTER 4

Miss Ashbrook jerked as if she had been slapped, and as she stared at the viscountess's lack of clothing, her eyes grew wider and wider.

At least the pain had lessened, though he doubted her ill-concealed shock and outrage were better. It was the pain which halted his tongue earlier, and a fierce regret burned through him that a young girl was ruined. Michael himself had never bedded an innocent, and the lovers he'd taken over the years were worldly women with passionate appetites. If Thomas had made it known that the girl he wanted to marry was with child, perhaps the outcome might very well be different. Now it was too damn late to do anything.

"Have you no sense of shame or propriety?" Miss Ashbrook demanded, glaring at the viscountess. "There is a child here, yet you flaunt yourself in such an unacceptable manner!"

Michael's admiration for Miss Ashbrook's mettle soared, and he didn't think it wise to point out a four-month old child would not have any recollection of this farce.

Laura, really Lady Meade, narrowed her eyes. "Such presumption, daring to speak to me in such a manner! Do you know who I am—"

"I do not give a fiddlestick who you are, and I will dare anything when it comes to my niece!"

"Laura," Michael said firmly, casting her a glance full of censure. "I will see you at the club later tonight. I apologize for not seeing you out."

Her cheeks mottled, and she nodded once before swirling away and slamming the door.

Miss Ashbrooke swiveled her gaze to him. "You take your wicked behavior to your home as well, your lordship?"

How scathingly and judgmental she sounded.

"Whatever I do in my home, Miss Ashbrook isn't your business."

She recoiled from his brusqueness. Then she frowned, looking worried. "Lizzie will need a nurturing and respectable home, your lordship, and from what I can see this is not it!"

"I am not an ogre," he said, his countenance admirably composed.

"You are a libertine! It is the middle of the day, …and you were cavorting!"

He decided to ignore this. "You may rest assured the child will be taken care of as is her due."

She worried her bottom lip with her teeth, clearly a nervous gesture. "Might…might I see her sometimes?" she asked, turning away her flushed countenance, and biting her lip.

That he had not expected. And it was as he peered closer at Miss Ashbrook, he detected a storm of emotions brewing in her eyes. She appeared tightly drawn as if any moment now, she would shatter.

"How do you propose to see her?"

Her throat worked on a swallow. "I've recently accepted a post as a governess to Lord Sanderson. I shall be in town for the foreseeable future. Perhaps on my off day…I…could take her to the park? Or sit with her and read?"

Her voice cracked on that last bit, but she held herself rigid, and Michael sensed she would soon be at the end of her rope.

"I have no objections," he said softly.

The sheen in her gaze shined brighter. "Very well, your lordship. There is a valise with all her clothing inside, and a letter of instructions for her wet nurse. If that is all, I shall see myself out until next time."

It was impossible to read her countenance. She walked over to the child, bent over her, and pressed a kiss to her forehead. Then Miss Ashbrook straightened, and without looking at him, hurried from the room as if the devil chased her.

The need to go after her blasted through Michael. He could not explain it, but something about her fragility in the moment before she fled compelled him to follow her. He went after her, hoping to catch her before a carriage took her away. What he would say, Michael had no notion.

He was unquestionably out of his senses.

Her heart felt as it was being ripped from her chest. Marianne rushed down the few steps which had led to the viscount's elegant townhouse and took deep, cleansing breaths. It did nothing to calm the tangle of emotions which knotted her chest—pain that her family might never see Lizzie again, anger at Papa for refusing to think of another plan that did not involve giving her away, fear that the viscount's wicked and licentious lifestyle might not be the best option for her niece. Could a man of his dissolute lifestyle even properly care for a child?

Marianne turned left and walked with quick steps along the cobbled walkway, grateful to see the area empty. After taking a few steps, it hit her that she was leaving Lizzie behind. A flash of wild grief gripped her.

It was Marianne who had cared for her these past several weeks for Lucy had sunk into a deep slump of melancholy and wept daily. It was Marianne who had bathed Lizzie, sang to her, took long walks with her in the woods, and it was Marianne who had convinced Papa Lizzie was too young to travel and to grant her a few more weeks at home.

And now, she was walking away from her. A harsh, ugly sob broke from her throat, and she faltered, unable to take another step. Tears coursed down her cheeks, and her shoulders shook as pain clawed from her stomach and escaped from her throat in a ragged gasp.

"Miss Ashbrook," a voice said from behind her.

She whirled around to see the viscount had followed her. "Your lordship!" Marianne tried to wipe away the evidence of her breakdown, to no avail.

The viscount stared at her, his eyes darkly contemplative. "Is everything quite well, Miss Ashbrook?"

To her frustration and humiliation, more tears spilled. Her stomach cramped; her eyes began to burn. "Lizzie… Lizzie…whenever she cries, if you would ask her nurse to sing to her, it will calm her," she gasped. "And she must sleep each night wrapped in her yellow blanket. It comforts her. And you mustn't be wild and wicked with her under your roof. You…you will have to adjust now that she is in your life. She will need a competent governess when she is much older, of course. One who will not demean her because of the circumstance of her birth."

The very idea of Lizzie suffering in such a manner made Marianne cry harder. "Her governess must be able to give instruction in the pianoforte, watercolor painting, arithmetic, needlework, and foreign languages. She should be loved and treated as if the circumstances of her birth were honorable. Lizzie should not suffer for the mistakes of her parents, but I fear the cruelty of society will not allow it to be so."

To her complete shock, the viscount took her hand and placed it atop his arm. "Walk back with me." Then he took her valise in his other hand.

Marianne did not understand why she followed him, only knowing she was too dispossessed of rational sense to arrive in such a state at Lord Sanderson's home for their meeting in an hour. It was only a few steps back to the viscount's house, and with discreet efficiency, he led her back to the drawing-room, past the butler and a few maids who gaped in an overly curious manner.

A handkerchief materialized, and she took it, wiped her cheeks. "I am so very mortified. I assure you, I am not normally a watering pot. I am quite sensible with my emotions, Papa has always said so," she said in a choked whisper.

"Don't be." There was a significant pause, and he said, "Did you attend a finishing school, Miss Ashbrook."

Marianne clutched the handkerchief in a tight grip and stared at the viscount. "I beg your pardon?"

He patiently repeated his question, and she stared at him as confusion twisted through her. "I have been most carefully educated by my mother, my father, who is the reverend of our parish, and my former governess Miss Robinson."

"And what were you so carefully instructed in?" he asked with an arched brow.

"I…how is this of any relevance?"

"Please, Miss Ashbrook, indulge me," he drawled with a slightly crooked smile.

She glanced away briefly, terribly uncomfortable at always noticing how handsome he was. "I was instructed in household management, pianoforte, Greek, Latin, French, and some Italian. Arithmetic, geography, and literature, of course."

"I would like to hire you to help me take care of Lizzie, as her governess. I should think you more than qualified for the post. You speak very well, you appear educated, and you are related to her. Miss Ashbrook, you will never be indifferent to her care and upbringing, that I am certain of though we have just met."

"That is absurd!"

"Why?"

"She does not need a governess until she is at least four years of age. Until then a wet nurse for feeding, and—"

"And *you*. I have no knowledge of children, much less a baby. You forget I am the wicked, unprincipled rake who owns a gambling club of ill repute. What do I have to offer her other than my wealth? I daresay if any child needs a governess at such a tender age it is Lizzie. One who will protect her from any foolish mistakes I might make…say bringing home a lover in the middle of the day."

She gasped. "You wouldn't dare!"

Unexpected deviltry danced in his eyes. "Surely not with you as her governess. I shall compensate you well, of course. Two hundred pounds for the year, with two off days for the week. And whenever you need to leave for a respite, you only need to inform me."

His generous offer was twice what Lord Sanderson had made. Marianne gaped at the viscount as if he had grown horns and a tail. Why would he do such a kindness? "What will people say?" she whispered. "I…you are unmarried and—"

"So is Lord Sanderson," he interposed smoothly, stepping scandalously close to her. "and you had been about to start working for the man. Society would not dare to speculate on the relationship between any lord and his employee."

Marianne, emotionally wrecked by everything—her father's anger, Lucy's pain, her mother's melancholy, the horrid journey, and the agony of leaving Lizzie made only a token of resistance before subsiding on to the viscount's shoulder and indulging in a burst of tears.

She was horrified at her lack of control but could not bring herself to stop crying. It took a few moments to realize that she was clasped in a comforting embrace with the man who had ruined her sister. Marianne jerked away from him, pressing a hand over her mouth. Never had she allowed another man so close to her person. When and how the viscount had sneaked past her defenses, she did not know.

As she stared at him, a searing flash of awareness burned through her. He lowered his lashes briefly, a faint flush seeped across his cheekbones, but she had seen it, a dark burn of hunger, one she had to interpret as desire for it had been so profound.

The viscount wanted her…the way a man wanted a woman. Marianne had never been the recipient of such a stare before…except for that night months' ago outside his club when he'd wanted to kiss her. Way down in her stomach, she felt an unknown ache. Shock scattered her thoughts, and a soft breath shuddered from between her lips. She had allowed him to comfort her, to be held against his body in an intimate embrace. How easy it had been for the charming scoundrel to slip under her careful guard. It only took a moment to lose everything—one's virginity, honor, and the trust and respect of her family. Lucy had fallen, Marianne would be an utter fool to allow the same fate to befall her, and by the same man!

The rejection of his offer hovered on her tongue, only waiting to be voiced. Lizzie chose that moment to release a thin wail, and Marianne walked over to her and gently took her from the well-padded basket. She was wet and more than likely hungry. As she stared at her niece, a rush of love blossomed through Marianne. She closed her eyes, pained at the very idea of leaving sweet Lizzie.

How can I not be here for you in any way that I can? No answer came, and Marianne stared at the viscount. "I accept," she murmured.

Something primal and entirely unsettling flashed in that dark-silver gaze of his, leaving her to wonder if she had just made the most perilous mistake a young lady of virtue could ever make—living unchaperoned under the roof of a man the newssheets called Viscount Wicked.

CHAPTER 5

Michael peered down at the laughing crowd, aloof from the general excitement which pulsed in the air. He scanned the faro and whist tables, the hazard, and the roulette wheel. It was a busy night, and every table on the floor was filled with ladies and gentlemen hoping to take home winnings from one of the tables or from the fights. Some climbed the staircase to the second floor and strolled with excitement in their steps toward the fighting club. There they placed even greater wagers on men who participated in the brutal sport of bare-knuckle brawling. He also had private rooms, where those with similar political affiliations could meet and have their vigorous discussion over cigar and brandy.

Dozens of tables were sprawled in an organized fashion, and at each table either cards were sliced and shuffled with artistic expertise, or dice danced between the roulette wheels to the spectators, who were holding their breath. A cheer went up from a table, and a man he recognized as Mr. Percy Stanton appeared dazed. Michael glanced at one of his men placed in the club at strategic points to ensure order at all times, and that there was no cheating, or harassment of the ladies who served champagne, whisky, or brandy on golden salvers.

One of his most ruthless enforcers—Dorian Martin—made a discreet signal with his hand. It seemed Mr. Stanton had won a fortune, at least one over five thousand pounds. No wonder the man appeared as if he did not know what to do with himself. It was unlikely he would ever see such a sum gained from his profession in his lifetime.

Michael had opened only recently his establishment to ladies and gentlemen of the genteel middle class. While some had frowned at this unprecedented move, his gambling den was still considered one of the golden halls, and in the caliber of Brooks, White's, and The Cocoa Tree, but because of the fighting den and the ballrooms, it had also garnered a reputation of wicked profligacy like many clubs in Soho Square.

Michael lifted his head slightly, and Dorian moved through the tables with stealthy elegance for such a large man. He approached Mr. Stanton and pointed him to stare up at Michael.

The man understood he was being summoned. Mr. Stanton appeared nervous as he climbed the winding grand staircase as fast as he could. When he reached Michael, he bowed.

He straightened and tugged at his cravat. "Lord Worsley, you wanted to speak with me?"

"I do. It is time for you to go home."

The man blanched. "Is it something I said or—"

"You did nothing wrong, Mr. Stanton, but as I understand it, you just won a small fortune. I've seen many men win a sizeable sum, and before they leave and invest it wisely, they continue gambling and lose it all. Drink a celebratory drink and go to the office on the second floor for a draft of your winnings. Go home. Pay your bills. Buy your wife something pretty. Put aside at least a quarter to your wife's portion or your child's inheritance. Then you can come back with the rest of it, if you wish, and try your luck again."

The man stared at him in astonishment. "My lord…I do not know what to say, I—"

"There is nothing to say, just do it," Michael said, lacing his voice with steel.

One of the greatest benefits he saw to his gambling establishment was the redistribution of wealth. Many men walked into his doors poor and struggling to survive within society and left with some measure of fortune to see them and their family comfortable for a few years. Many also came and lost thousands, and Michael had made it a policy to cut men off who gambled too recklessly whether they be influential dukes or a mere barrister.

He did not want those who had lost everything to go home, place a pistol in their mouths, and blow their brains out. A dark feeling swept over him as the memory of how he had found his father in his library ten years' ago blackened his thoughts. Brushing it aside, he turned back to observe the floor, while Mr. Stanton bowed and hurried away, a definite jaunt in his step.

Dark blue and silver drapes to the left of the tables were drawn open to reveal a ballroom. A quick glance at his pocket watch showed it to be ten pm. The twenty-piece orchestra started the waltz, and many ladies and gentlemen, who had hovered watching others play, swept onto the dance floor, moving to the music in a far more scandalous manner than they would ever dare in a public ballroom.

A dark blond head passing below a chandelier by one

of the hazard tables drew his attention. Thomas. He watched as his brother flirted with a masked lady, before leading her onto the dance floor. Unlike the other patrons, he kept a respectable distance, even when the lady tried to close the space between them. His brother danced for a while, before making the rounds and greeting a few of his cronies. He glanced up, and upon spying Michael, Thomas lifted his fingers to his forehead in a pastiche of a military salute.

A rush of exasperated affection twisted through Michael. Only seven years separated them in age, Thomas being three and twenty to Michael's thirty. Yet at times he felt like his bloody father and not his older brother. He lifted his chin, indicating for his brother to meet him in the large office on the second floor.

Michael arrived at the office he shared with Thomas and poured brandy in a glass as he waited for his brother to arrive. He sat behind his large oak desk, the second such desk in the room, and leaned back in a high wingback chair. It had only been yesterday Miss Ashbrook had barged into his life with baby Lizzie. And since then, at the oddest times, Michael was blasted with the oddest sense of panic, before he brushed it aside and drew upon the resolve which had seen him taking over a gambling den at twenty years old.

Employing Miss Ashbrook may have been in equal measure the smartest and stupidest thing he could have done in the circumstances. She was the most suited person to rear the babe, being acquainted with the child from birth and being her aunt. But the way Miss Ashbrook affected him, being under his roof must be a recipe for some great disaster. But he was resolved to be an utter gentleman to the only woman who had affected him for some time.

After Miss Ashbrook had agreed to stay on as Lizzie's governess, he had moved with grim efficiency to set all the proper things in motion. He had introduced her to the staff along with Lizzie and had arranged for the housekeeper to place her in comfortable quarters. His townhouse only had eight bedrooms, and she had been given the one closest to him. Michael had barely slept, knowing the only woman who had roused him in months slept just a connecting door away.

Ruthless thoughts of seduction had danced in his brain, and he had padded downstairs in the dead of night to his exercise room, to practice boxing moves for hours. With his muscles aching and sweat dampening his hair, he had fallen into a deep and restful sleep, thankfully without any provocative dreams.

The door opened, and Thomas strolled in with a wide smile. "Viscountess Meade is outside these doors, asking after you. I told her our meeting would only be a few minutes, and the lady has determined to wait."

At his lack of response, Thomas arched a brow. "Is all well? You appear more serious than usual."

Michael indicated the sofa closest to his desk. With a nonchalant shrug, Thomas lowered himself in the plush depths and stared at his brother. Thomas was a handsome lad, very similar in appearance to Michael for they both possessed their father's dark blond hair, gray eyes, and lean build.

"I can tell you have something on your mind."

"Tell me about Lucy Ashbrook," Michael said softly.

Thomas paled, and his throat worked on a swallow. At this moment he looked like a young lad of three and twenty on the cusp of discovering the world, not the savvy genius who did the club's bookkeeping.

"Lucy?" he asked faintly, his gaze scanning the room as if he expected her to appear.

"Yes. Lucy Ashbrook."

Thomas raked trembling fingers through his hair and closed his eyes for several moments. "She…Lucy…how do you know of her?"

"I gather you do not remember mentioning her to me once?"

At his brother's bewildered look, Michael continued, "Ah…clearly you do not. You were in your cups, heavily I might add, and you asked me to allow you to marry her. I asked if you were afflicted and why would you think to marry a girl with such little connections, and you made no answer. That was the only time I heard you mention her. When I saw you the next morning, you did not mention her, and I was foolish enough to simply shrug it off as you being foxed."

Thomas shook his head, dazedly. "I do not recall that conversation, Michael."

"Tell me about her."

"She…she was a girl I love…*loved*."

Michael leaned back in the wing back chair, assessing his brother. A dark throb of anger pulsed through him. "And that is all you have to say."

Thomas jerked to his feet and started pacing. "I met her last Season at Lady Goodall's soirée. She was sitting in the garden and seemed very unhappy at the time I approached her, and we…we struck up a friendship. We were never formally introduced, but I contrived to meet her several times. Lucy was charming and pretty and…so vibrant."

"There was no mention of Lord Thomas paying attention to any society miss. The scandal sheets made no speculation about you."

"I was not publicly courting her," Thomas snapped, an edge of frustration in his tone. "She is the daughter of a country vicar. Her manners were charming, but she did not meet the requirements to be my wife!"

A painful silence fell in the office.

"But she met the requirement for you to ruin her chances of ever securing a match of her own. She was worth bedding, but not much more?"

Thomas blanched, faltered in his pacing, and narrowed his eyes. "What knowledge do you have of Lucy and me?"

"Sit!" Michael's voice cut through the room like sharpened steel.

His brother stiffened, but he made his way to the sofa and lowered his frame. His pose was tight with tension, and his lips were flat and unsmiling.

"I believed I told you never to take an innocent to your bed!"

Thomas could not meet his eyes and looked somewhere above Michael's shoulder.

"A young lady showed up at my townhouse yesterday. With a child she claims is mine."

He snapped his gaze to Michael's. "Good God!"

"That young lady is Miss Marianne Ashbrook. The mother of the child is Lucy Ashbrook."

Thomas understood the situation immediately. His mouth worked, but no word came forth for several moments. "Lucy and I…we have a child?" he asked in horrified accents.

"Yes."

Thomas stared, his eyes welling, then he glanced away, evidently fighting for composure. "Is she married…is Lucy married?"

"No," Michael said icily. "Your child is a bastard in the eyes of society and the law."

Thomas flinched then dropped his forehead in his palms, his elbows resting on his thighs. "I promised her I would marry her," he said in a tortured voice. "I loved her."

"Why did you not come to me when you learned of her delicate state?"

A derisive laugh came from his brother. "Would you have given your blessing?"

"Do you really need it to marry a woman you said you loved…and one who carried your child?"

Thomas was silent for a very long time, and Michael waited, granting him space to untangle his thoughts.

"No, I suppose that should be the last thing I should have been worried about. I…" he lifted his face from his palms. "When she told me, I was frightened. In the history of our family, no-one has married a lady with such unimportant connections and fortune. I went to my home and drank myself into a stupor for days. When my head was clear I felt certain I wanted to be with Lucy, I went to the park. She was not there. I hoped she would be there."

Michael took the letter from his pocket, placed it atop his desk, and pushed it toward his brother. "She waited for you in that park for several days."

Thomas reached for it and read it. At one point, he flinched, and as he refolded it and placed it in his pocket, his hand trembled.

"You told her you were Viscount Worsley."

His brother flushed, shame darkening his eyes. "I…I took her here one night, and I had wanted her to believe I was more important than a second son. She had the liveliest sense of humor, but after a few hours together, I still could not bear to tell her it was my older brother who held the title."

"You were a damn fool and a blackguard," Michael

said without mercy. "Now there is a four-month old child in my home. What do you intend to do?"

"I cannot afford for a word of this to reach Lord Kenwood. It would be an embarrassment to the earl's family and to Lady Sarah. Our wedding is in five months, and I want to avoid a scandal."

"And how do you plan to do that?"

He rubbed the back of his neck. "George found himself in a similar situation a few months back with his mistress."

George was Lord Sutton, a young viscount who had a reckless heart for racing and was his brother closest friend.

"His lady dove gave birth to his child a few months' ago. They placed in her the most appropriate orphanage. Society is none the wiser about it, and the place is very tip-top, and the child will receive a proper education."

"And you wish to do the same with Elizabeth?"

A flash of surprise and wonder crossed his brother's face. "It is a girl then."

To that, Michael made no reply, and his brother asked, "Do you know where Lucy was all this time?"

"You did not know?"

"No. If I knew I would like to believe I would have chased Lucy and asked her father for her hand. But that is in the past now, and I am now engaged. All the announcements have been made and…" Thomas stopped speaking.

"She lives in disgrace in Wiltshire with her family. She is not permitted to keep the child. Her father also wished to place Elizabeth in an orphanage."

Thomas swallowed. "Many people have left their by-blows in the care of such an establishment. They have done so for years."

In his brother's eyes, he saw guilt and deep shame.

"You could also claim her."

Thomas winced. "The scandal would be rife throughout the *ton*. And Lady Sarah does not deserve such speculations into her life. She is a very genteel lady and tends to swoon at the slightest provocation."

"You will also make provision for Miss Lucy discreetly. A cottage, at least four bedrooms, and a yearly portion that will see her living comfortably." Michael could easily settle the matter himself, but Thomas needed to face some of the responsibility for his dishonor. "Meet with our solicitor immediately and see it done."

Michael stood. "The child will stay in my care until further notice."

His brother stared at him in astonishment. "Why?"

A bite of anger curled through him. "Because she is your daughter and my niece."

Thomas flushed and looked away but made no reply.

"I've hired Doris Chambers to be her wet nurse."

Thomas's eyes widened. "The widow who works downstairs serving drinks?"

Doris had given birth to her own child four months' ago and had always seemed discomfited to work in the club. But desperate to provide for her family of three children she had plodded onward. She had been pleased when he had extended the offer earlier and had made her way to his town home with instructions. "Yes."

Thomas's lips parted as if he would dare to think to question Michael's decision but clearly thought better of it.

"Thank you, Michael," he said gruffly.

He opened the door for his brother to depart. "I did not do it for you, never deceive yourself into believing that."

Shockingly that was the truth. Miss Ashbrook's wide wounded eyes which had been filled with such anxiety and fear for her niece's care and safety had been the primary reason Michael had decided an orphanage would never do, even the best of them. Many in society cast their bastards away with little care to their upbringing. Gentlemen were judged to be crass and vulgar if they claimed their by-blows, and many hid their children in orphanages. He believed if he had informed Miss Ashbrook he would take Elizabeth to such a home, she would have contrived to run away with the child and do everything in her power to care for her. To his way of thinking, if she had been able to do that, she would never have approached an unprincipled libertine like himself for his assistance.

He had hovered yesterday, like a dark shadow, watching as she had boiled milk and water and dribbled it with a handkerchief for Lizzie to suck on. The care Miss Ashbrook had taken when she bathed her and then put her down to sleep, softly singing to her. Her love had been painful to observe, and he had melted away to his chamber savagely cursing the delightful Miss Ashbrook for bravely daring to live in his lair.

He would eventually take her and damn them both to hell, his resistance to her allure was very fragile. He had been trying to drive from his mind how much she enflamed his body. Having found himself repeatedly reacting to the sight of her tending his beautiful tiny niece. His self-control had never troubled him with such force before. Michael closed the door firmly behind his brother's exit and pressed his forehead to the door. *No…I'll not seduce her. I am not ruled by my damn cock as if I was an untried boy.* He would not be a man ruled by any vice, even that of fornication. He was nothing like his father who had lost his fortune at the gambling tables and who had so despaired of living without wealth and his favorite estate, that he had killed himself without thought for his two young sons or his loving wife.

A sharp hiss escaped him, and he ruthlessly disciplined all the fire of lust and strange emotions twisting inside until they were quashed back down and no longer troubled his thoughts. While he was a man of strong appetites, he had never given himself over to any vice, and he would not start now. The situation might be laughable if his cock didn't ache so much.

Opening the door, he paused to see Laura sauntering toward him, dressed in a very provocative red gown with a very revealing neckline. Nothing stirred within him, and he frowned.

"Michael darling," she said, pressing her body against his and twining her hand around his neck. She trailed a sharp nail across his cheek and down into his neckcloth.

He untangled himself from her arms, "Laura, we will not be lovers."

Her lips parted in shock. Possibly that had been too blunt and badly done by him, but his patience was at an end.

A petulant pout settled on her lips. "I was naked in your drawing room yesterday!"

"And we were interrupted."

Her eyes flashed with anger…and once again with a challenge. Whispers had started to make the rounds that he hadn't had a lover in a while. Instead of the mockery he expected, ladies anticipated being the one to break his dry spell. They had dug into their arsenal of seductive wiles and had been competing to be the one who would succeed in seducing him. To become the Viscount Wicked's mistress, even if not acknowledged as such, had a certain cachet worth fighting to achieve.

He knew his reputation as a lover had been secretly

whispered about and he had been slightly amused to discover that he was considered inventive and superbly depraved. Yesterday he had contemplated taking Laura to his bed. She had been the boldest of the coterie, she had shown up at his home, and in the middle of taking refreshments closed the door to the drawing-room and started to undress. Her boldness and creativity had momentarily captivated him, but by the time she had taken off her stockings, he had been bored. Miss Ashbrook's barging into his house had been a timely intervention.

"Is it because of that mousey—"

"Do not dare," he interjected with icy civility. "I assure you would not like being the brunt of my displeasure."

The viscountess hesitated, flushing slightly.

"If you will allow me to escort you to the lower floors," he said, holding out his arm.

Though her lips pinched in annoyance, she accepted. She forced a glittering smile as they made their way down into the laughter, chatter, smoke, and general debauchery which no longer had the power to entice him to play.

CHAPTER 6

The faint creak of a floorboard had Marianne sitting up in bed and clutching the sheet to her throat. She listened for a few more moments, then released a slow breath. This was her third night under the wicked viscount's roof, and she was finding it just as difficult falling asleep as it had been yesterday and the day before.

The viscount's townhouse had a stone façade and climbed four stories above the lower ground floor. It was very grand and tastefully furnished. The lower floors held a large and elegantly appointed drawing-room, a smaller parlor stylishly decorated, a breath-taking library, a palatial music room, the viscount's study, and an impressive ballroom that opened onto small gardens. Lizzie would be quite happy growing up in this home, and Marianne imagined his country estates were even grander.

A fire blazed in the hearth, and the exquisite chamber she had been assigned was delightfully warm. Marianne felt wretched and elated to be in the viscount's town home. To be so near to Lizzie every day should be such a wonderful joy, but deceiving her family haunted her thoughts. She'd convinced herself it was proper, for she was gainfully employed, and it was quite common for female employees and servants to work for an unmarried gentleman without undue speculation.

She told herself society would truly never think for a moment, something improper might happen. It was too inconceivable that a gentleman would dally with someone so far below him in station. Marianne was not so sure that they would consider living under Viscount Worsley's roof so innocent. The man had a reputation for wicked debauchery and she feared there might be some whispering about her presence in his household. Especially as Elizabeth might be believed to be her own. How had Lucy believed this man would have married her? Upon the heel of that thought, an even deeper discomfort curled through her.

The viscount had denied that he was the father, and for a moment, she had believed him. Marianne closed her eyes briefly, cursing her naïveté, before pushing the sheet from her body and scrambling from the bed. It was pointless to remain in bed and drive herself mad with questions she had no answers to or worried about them, for they would still be present in the morning.

A good book was what she needed to help her to sleep, and the cursory tour she had been given by the housekeeper had shown a very large and wonderfully stocked library on the second floor. She donned her wrapper, took up a candlestick, then opened the door. Her footsteps were silent as she headed down the hall, toward the chamber Lizzie shared with Doris, the nursemaid the viscount had procured in one afternoon. She was a plain-looking but quite amiable young widow, she had an infant of her own that was still quite young and seemed to have already fallen in love with Lizzie. Marianne had been impressed with his efficiency but hadn't been able to find it in her heart to praise the man. Pushing open the door carefully, Marianne crept forward and peered down into the crib. Her niece slept on her stomach, her tiny hand pillowed beneath her rosy cheek.

A dart of hunger quivered through her heart, and she tenderly tugged the blanket higher over the baby. Before Lizzie had been born, Marianne hadn't given much thought to her future or to having a family of her own. Though Mama had spoken fondly of her hopes that Marianne would marry a gentleman from the small town, no-one had captured her heart or attention. The local doctor had called upon her a few times, and they had taken several walks together, but he had left her frightfully uninspired.

Marianne had felt a very deep hunger to leave the town of Biddleton and to explore more of England, especially to experience town life. When their aunt on their father's side, a baroness in her own right, had offered to take one of the Ashbrook girls to London to explore some of its charm and social events; Marianne had allowed Lucy's pleading to sway her from insisting as the elder daughter living at home she should be the one to travel to town.

With a sigh, she pushed aside her regrets from allowing Lucy to leave. Ensuring she did not disturb Doris's sleep, Marianne gently closed the door behind her and stepped into the hall.

The deceit she felt guilty about lying to her father as to where she was living and how she had disposed of Elizabeth weighed heavily on her heart, yet Marianne knew she could not take him into her full confidence. Papa had been very unwilling to allow her to spread her wings and leave Biddleton, he had struggled with his desire to keep her safely at home. Only the financial struggle of the family to cope on his tiny stipend had induced him to agree with her plans. She'd had to gently remind him that she was three and twenty, her dowry of one hundred pounds would not attract any eligible suitor, and she could not live forever with her parents in their charming cottage.

There was more to life than an idyllic existence in the tiny town of Biddleton. And the first step to discovering it had been to find a modicum of independence through employment befitting her station.

Hurrying down the hall, she entered the library happy to see that it was empty, and that a pleasant fire still blazed in the hearth. The clock on the mantle showed it to be three in the morning, and based on the previous nights' experience, she did not expect the viscount to return home for another few hours.

From the shelves, she selected *The Castle of Otranto* and made her way back to her room. Her steps slowed when she noticed that one of the doors was slightly ajar, flames flickered and danced inside casting shadows, and there was a scratching sound. She glanced up and down the hallway, which now appeared menacingly dark. Gripping her candlestick even tighter, she made to move on to her room, but dreadful curiosity got the better of her. Marianne eased the ajar door open a bit more and peered inside the room.

She stared in astonishment at the viscount. He was in a state of dishevelment and seated on the floor, a knife and something wooden in his hand.

"Are you going to stay there and stare? Or will you come in."

She gasped softly, wondering how he knew she was there. Marianne withdrew, and lowered her hand from the doorknob, hating how unsettled she suddenly felt. Yet her feet or her mind did not carry her away, and she hovered on the threshold.

"I know you are still there," came a soft, amused murmur.

Marianne could feel a flush creeping up her cheeks, and she wished she could control her reaction. Taking a deep breath, she pushed the door open wider, careful to ensure it remained ajar. Not that it was much of a protection, but nonetheless it comforted her.

The walls of the room were decorated in a very pretty purple and silver wallpaper. No drapes had been put up as yet, and the beauty of the moonlight beamed into the room directly on the viscount. The floor was bare of carpeting, but the dark hardwood floor gleamed as if it had been recently polished and the scent of lemon wax was redolent on the air. A large and quite handsome peach crib trimmed with muslin and lace with a canopy to match was in the center of the room. And a few feet from it was a swinging cradle.

Her heart trembled. "You are preparing a nursery," she whispered.

The viscount turned around. "Come and see."

She glanced over her shoulder at the open doorway, before walking over to a small rosewood table where she rested the candlestick and book. Then she went over to him and lowered herself onto the floor, folding her legs beneath her in a similar fashion as the viscount.

There was an array of carved animals before her, eight in total. She took up one of the animals and peered at it. "What is this?"

"That is a lion," he muttered, still fiercely concentrated on the image he was carving. He wielded that small knife with such dexterity she stared amazed as the trunk of an elephant made itself evident.

"You are making these for Lizzie?"

He grunted softly. "Yes. I know she will not be able to play with them now…but they will be here with her. I have been thinking to paint them, but my skills with the paintbrush are sadly lacking."

He chose that moment to look up and smile in that lopsided fashion of his. An alarming sensation tumbled low in her stomach, and she lowered her gaze to the array of carved animals. It occurred to her he must have been in this room for hours. "I walked by earlier on my way to the library…and I did not notice someone was in here."

"I opened the door slightly when I heard you padding by."

Her gaze flew to his, and there was a very wicked glint in his silver gaze.

"You are outrageous," she muttered, unsure what to do with that knowledge. It was as if a wolf had laid a trap and she had waltzed right into it with her inquisitiveness.

"And perhaps a little bit charming?"

"I wouldn't dare ever say so," she said with a sniff. "I will admit your carvings are exquisite."

An odd silence fell between them, and they stared at each other.

"One day, I shall take her to see these animals in the flesh. I am sure she will find them of interest. When my father took my brother and me to the Menagerie at Exeter Change years' ago, we did not wish to leave."

Something warm and heady unfurled inside Marianne. The viscount spoke of Lizzie being in his life years from now. That meant he intended to keep her home with him and not banish her to some orphanage or boarding school. It spoke to the kindness of his character which she had not expected. Similar to the kindness he had shown in offering her the post of governess so she could be close to Lizzie.

"We could take Lizzie to the London Zoo in Regent's Park. Many of the animals which had belonged to the Royal Menagerie were sent there—Lions, tigers, wolves, leopards, and monkeys. I believe she would like that."

A giddy sense of happiness rushed through her. It was heartwarming that the viscount wanted her to be a part of Lizzie's experiences. Marianne reached over and picked up a carved monkey. "I read the London Zoo is not opened to the public."

"If you wish to attend, I will see it done."

She supposed that meant he had the wealth and connections for her to gain admittance. Marianne wasn't certain how she felt about such vaunting of privilege, but she was intrigued. "I've never seen any of the exotic animals," she murmured. "I've read of them, but I shan't like seeing such beautiful spirits caged."

"Ah…a very similar feeling that my brother and I shared when we were taken to the menagerie. I recall some screams on my part about how cruel they were and being scolded most severely by our father for shaming the family with our odious display of vulgarity."

His tone was mild, but deviltry danced in his eyes. "Would you like a drink, Miss Ashbrook?"

"A drink?" she parroted and then noticed the decanter of amber liquid and glass to his right on the floor. Her heart gave a patter in warning. "Of course not!" she said, hating that she flushed. How gauche and unworldly she must appear to a man of his experience.

His gaze kissed over her face in a too intimate fashion. "I detect a measure of guilt," he drawled provocatively. "Could it be that the reverend's daughter has been secretly indulging?"

Marianne laughed, startling herself. "Perhaps once or

twice, my sisters and I have pilfered a taste of my Papa's port. He *would* be aghast should he ever discover."

"How shockingly improper," he said drolly. "You have more than one sister, Miss Ashbrook."

"Yes, there are six of us in total."

"Six girls?"

"Papa wasn't fortunate enough to be blessed with a son. But it was wonderful growing with sisters."

"And you are the eldest?"

"I…no, Victoria has that honor. I am the second daughter." She thought about her sister, who had left home over two years to travel the continent and was recently engaged. "Victoria is daring and hated being trapped in Biddleton. Papa's younger brother and his wife decided to take a tour of Europe. They are childless and had been wanting to make that trip for some years. Victoria was old enough to decide on her own, and somehow, she convinced Uncle Walton and Aunt Lydia to take her with them. The last letter I received from her, they were living in Brussels, and she is engaged to Captain Warwick Spencer of the British navy and is having a wonderful time."

"You sound envious."

She lifted startled eyes to find him staring at her with astonishing intensity.

"I am most certainly not jealous!" Yet there was a part of her that wished she was with her sister, seeing more of the world. "Perhaps a smidgen," she admitted with a smile. "Biddleton is a good home but also frightfully boring at times. There are so many long walks one can take…"

"I've heard from a few friends of late that marriage can be exhilarating," he said with a good deal of skepticism.

"Are you asking me why I am unmarried, your lordship?"

"Yes," he murmured with that slight crook of his lips.

"You are young, perhaps about two and twenty and *frightfully* beautiful."

"Three and twenty," she said, staring at him, not liking the unexpected flutter in her stomach. Viscount Wicked, a connoisseur of pretty ladies, thought her beautiful. Nonsense, but deep inside, something purred.

"I've always thought I would only marry a man who complimented my character, temper, and understanding."

"Ah, and such paragon of goodness might not be found in Biddleton?"

"Has your lordship assumed my character and temper is one of the loftiest of virtues?"

Interest gleamed in the dark silver of his gaze. "Pray tell, is there a smidgen of mischief there?"

There was an undercurrent of something decidedly wicked in his tone. A kiss of warning quivered down her spine, and her heart increased its tempo. "Perhaps, I shall hardly own to it to a man of your proclivities. Papa always said one should not admit a weakness aloud considering the devil might be listening."

Amusement leaped into his eyes, and if she were not mistaken, admiration. She felt struck through by the sight of it.

"Of course, I am clearly Satan, that vile tempter." Only the faintest tremor in his voice betrayed the humor he found in the situation.

"I know it was very poor-spirited of me to imply that you are the devil."

"Think nothing of it," he replied with admirable gravity.

She was now enjoying herself quite considerably, and acting on the impulse she leaned forward, grabbed the decanter, and poured some of the amber liquid into a glass. Then she took a careful sip. A wave of fire engulfed her entire body, and she sucked in a harsh breath. "What vile drink is this?"

His lips moved, not quite a smile. "Brandy."

"It is dreadful," she said, handing him the glass.

Her heart tripped alarmingly when he tipped it to his mouth, his lips edging the rim of the glass exactly where hers had been. It suddenly looked and felt shockingly intimate. The soft warning exploded into distressing alarm. She sank her teeth into her bottom lip, an awful nervous gesture, and his predatory gaze lingered on her lips. A frown marred his brow, and he looked away from her. With a single swallow, he downed the contents of the glass and placed it on the floor with a decided *click*.

Marianne stood, uncertain about the sudden tension in the room. "It is a beautiful nursery, my lord," she said. "I shall now retire to bed."

"Thank you for the company, Miss Ashbrook," he replied, his tone carefully blank. "The interlude was delightful."

She dipped into a quick curtsy, collected her book and the candlestick and hurried from the room, entirely conscious that his eyes followed. Once in the hallway, Marianne released a deep breath. She had been in his presence for at least thirty minutes, and not once had she recalled to mind he was the dishonorable bounder who had ruined her sister. Silently berating herself for her foolishness, she entered her room and set down the book and candlestick on the small vanity. Marianne shrugged from her robe and climbed into bed all thoughts of reading gone from her mind.

"Of course, snakes will be charming," she muttered to herself. "That is how they can trick people into ruin." Except the viscount had only presented himself as kind, quite thoughtful of her needs, and just a little bit wicked and charming.

Settling among her pillows and tugging the sheets to her chin, a peculiar disquiet filled Marianne's heart. *I mustn't like him beyond what is polite and proper*, she silently reminded herself as she fell into a deep slumber.

Except for the first time in her life, Marianne dreamed of kissing a man, and *of course*, it was the wicked viscount.

CHAPTER 7

Dearest Marianne,

I do hope you are well, and Lizzie too. I've thought of her often, and my heart breaks each day she is away from me. I also received your letter, and I am even happier to know she will be raised with the privilege of being the daughter of Lord Worsley. This gives me hope that I might see her in the future, even if it will be painful to see her father. A solicitor, Mr. Archibald Turner, on behalf of Lord Worsley, visited us in Biddleton. At first, Papa was angry at his unannounced visit and his intentions, but Mama calmed Father's anger, and we were all able to meet civilly. Mr. Turner provided me with this new location to write to you, and I am astonished it is not the previous address of Lord Sanderson which you provided. I do hope everything is well, and I trust in time you will inform me why you are at a different house. I know you are safe because you were always so sensible, as Papa often praised you for your common sense.

Now onto my news, Mr. Turner has informed me that a house will be purchased for me, and I am to receive a sum of one thousand pounds yearly until I am married. Papa at first refused but then came around after a couple hours. I cannot credit what changed his mind, but I am forever grateful. I was given the choice of where to live, and I picked Bath where I will move by next week and assume widowhood. I have decided to call myself Mrs. Lucy Elliot. I will be able to hire a cook, a housekeeper, a lady's maid, and still live in comfort. I promise I shall be very circumspect in my behavior and the society I keep company with. I am no longer interested in love or any gentleman! For the first time in months, I feel so hopeful that my future might not be so dreary. I daresay I will try my hand at writing a gothic novel as I have always wanted to, and the best place to do that is Bath.

I will send my address to you soon, and I do hope you will visit. I look forward to hearing from you.

Your sister, Lucy.

Marianne folded the letter, opening the drawer of the small writing desk in her room and slipped it inside. "Oh Lucy, I am so very grateful you seem happy," she whispered, then smiled.

Deep melancholy had gripped her sister after the birth of Lizzie, and nothing her sisters had done had been able to rouse Lucy's spirits. She had spent days abed crying, unable to even walk the baby in the woods for a breath of fresh air. Papa's continual disappointment and unforgiving attitude had not helped the situation. No doubt Papa had changed his mind because of their mother's influence, and surely, he would see that this was a chance to secure Lucy's future even if he hated the way it had come about. Marianne could picture her father on his knees, praying and trying to justify the decision of allowing Lucy to take some restitution from her debaucher. It would wrack his conscience dearly.

Marianne pushed back her chair, looking down on her clothing as she stood. She had made herself some plain gowns when she had been planning to go as a governess, and although she longed for the prettier clothes that society ladies could afford, she knew they fitted her station. She smoothed down the drab skirts of the dress she had chosen to wear that day and made her way from her room toward the nursery. Lizzie slept peacefully, no doubt sated from her recent feeding, and her walk in the park. For the last eight days since they had moved into the viscount's home, they had developed a routine. After Doris attended to the baby each morning, Marianne would take Lizzie for a walk in the perambulator, sometimes pushing her all the way to the small but quaint and elegant bookstore nearby. They would return home for her next feeding, and then afterward, Marianne would sit with her in the nursery and read to her before putting her down for her sleep. This allowed Doris to spend some time with her own children, who were now living with her sister.

The viscount was often absent from the townhouse, and when he was present, he stayed in his study. Their paths had crossed a few times, and he was very polite, warm even, but there had been no repeat of how they had conversed that night in the nursery.

Marianne enjoyed her days of walking and reading with Lizzie, but at times she felt awfully bored. For the last few nights, she would peer from her window as the viscount left the house in his elegant and well-sprung carriage dressed in the first stare of fashion. She supposed he went to his club or some societal event or perhaps to a mistress. Marianne had no notion of when he returned home, and would only chance upon him in the days, sometimes in the nursery with Lizzie in his arms.

The nursery turned out to be a bright, cheerful room, sunny and airy, and tastefully decorated and furnished. Truly a room fit for a little princess, and it had all been done by the viscount in a few days. His caring for Lizzie and attention to details warmed Marianne to him as nothing else could. The very sight of them together always filled Marianne's heart with a peculiar longing, and she would always melt away whenever he spied her.

She glided down the curved staircase. Perhaps today she would sup in the formal dining room instead of requesting a tray in her room. Anything different to break the tedium and silence of the evenings. It astonished her to realize how much of her time had been occupied with helping her family at the vicarage, or her mother as she made the rounds to call upon their parishioners in Biddleton.

Outside of helping Doris to care for Lizzie, there was simply little for Marianne to do. The music room had become her favorite room in the large, four-story townhouse, and it was to there she headed. A fire was always lit, and the light cream-colored wallpaper that contrasted with the darker furnishings gave a welcoming atmosphere. But it was the exquisitely crafted grand pianoforte that commanded her interest.

"May I take your hat and coat, Mr. St. Ives," the butler said.

At the foot of the stairs, she faltered and glanced down the hallway. *Mr. St. Ives?* This person was related to the viscount.

"Is she here?" the voice demanded. "Is Miss Ashbrook here?"

Marianne frowned, walking towards the source of that inquiry. They met somewhere in the middle of the hallway, and when the man saw her, he gaped.

"Lucy?"

Marianne froze, a sense of disbelief filling her veins. There had been such pain and wonder in the man's tone just now. She assessed him, uncaring that she did so in an unladylike manner. This man looked like a softer version to the viscount. Younger, cheeks more rounded, chin weaker, but still very handsome. A great pressure swelled in her chest, shortening her breath. Knowledge suddenly bloomed through her, for this young man, had a closer resemblance to the baby sleeping above stairs. "I am not Lucy," she managed to say.

"Of course not," he said with a flush. "Forgive me. I knew that, it is just the resemblance between you both is very striking. But I can now see a clear difference. You… you are a little shorter and…ah…forgive my impertinence. I am the honourable Thomas St. Ives. The viscount is my older brother."

"Lord Worsley is not here." She thought it prudent to point out.

Mr. St. Ives raked his fingers through his hair. "I came to see you. May we withdraw to the drawing-room for privacy, please."

She nodded, a multitude of questions tumbling through her thoughts. Once in the drawing-room, she turned to face him, clasping her fingers together across her middle.

"I…forgive my lack of manners," he said with an attempt at a charming smile. "I am Thomas St. Ives, Lord Worsley is my brother." He swallowed as if thinking about what to say.

"You are Lizzie's father," she said, cutting straight to the heart of her suspicion.

He closed his eyes briefly, then scrubbed a hand over his face. "I…I am."

Marianne did not understand the relief which pierced her, but the single thought which eclipsed all others was that she had not dreamed wickedly of kissing the man who had ruined her sister. But Thomas being here presented another fear. "Are you here to take Lizzie away?"

"Good God, no!"

How utterly aghast he sounded, and she stared at him in astonished disbelief.

"I…I wanted to ask about Lucy. I tried to stay away, I did, but I am haunted every night by the memories of our time together," he said with surprising frankness.

Marianne recalled the loss of hope she'd seen in her sister, and still the desperate love which had lingered for this deceitful man.

"Will you please tell me how Lucy is?"

"Are you to marry her?"

"I…no, of course not!"

Pain and disgust hammered at her and Marianne barely managed to maintain her calm composure. "Are you already married?"

"No. I fear it is frightfully complicated. I am recently affianced to the daughter of an earl, and it was publicly announced. I…just wanted to ask after Lucy."

"No," she said quietly. "Any news about my sister must come from her directly. That means you will have to face her and explain why you did not keep your promise."

A spasm of anguish crossed his face. "I see. I thank you for your time, Miss Ashbrook."

He turned and walked away, and when he had also crossed the threshold, she asked, "Will you see Lizzie?"

He faltered, his shoulders stiffened, then he clipped, "No." And disappeared.

Her mother had often instilled that a young lady should never show an excess of emotions, so Marianne breathed deeply to calm the need to race after that odious man and blister his ears. She rushed from the drawing-room and made her way up the stairs to her chamber, where she flung herself onto the comfortable bed. The knowledge of Lord Worsley not being Lizzie's father, but her uncle, and his beyond kind and tender actions toward her, nonetheless caused a broad smile of astonishment to twist Marianne's lips. And filled her heart with warmth. She composed a letter to her father in her thoughts;

Dear Papa,

I must confess to you I am not working as a governess for Lord Sanderson, but Viscount Worsley. Nor did I deliver Lucy to the orphanage you had selected, but to the man I thought to be her father. He is not vile or wicked or mean-spirited. The opposite. He is a charmer of course, but he is very kind, beyond what I expected of a man of his reputation. Papa, I think of him daily…and even in the nights when I sleep, to my abject frustration I dream of the viscount kissing me. I taste his lips, a mix of coffee and brandy I might imagine and perhaps a hint of wickedness that will see me surrendering…

With a groan she rolled over and pressed her face into the pillow. It was beyond silly that she should think of the viscount in such an improper manner! Sighing, she sat up. "A long walk to clear my thoughts is what I need," she whispered, stood and collected her shawl, hat, and gloves. It was a fine afternoon for walking, despite the sharp wind blowing.

Soon Marianne strolled down the avenue of Mayfair assessing the discontent worming through her heart. Being here in town, at the Viscount's home, and seeing him with Lizzie had awoken a powerful hunger in Marianne's heart. Yet it confounded her to try and untangle exactly what it was that she wanted. Her thoughts seemed so raveled together as if a kitten had been playing in her embroidery silks, but it was not a kitten tied up in silks that she needed to release from its bindings. No, she was the one secured tightly by threads, and they already bound her to the satin tongue of Viscount Wicked. Wickedness was plentiful within the gentle purr of his voice, its very softness lulling her into dreams she knew would always be unfulfilled. Common sense discouraged her, forcing her to doubt that the Viscount could ever fit into her dreams, for he was a leopard who would never change his spots.

Her gaze skipped over a few fashionably dressed women pushing perambulators. Another walking arm in arm with a gentleman, parasols opened to protect their delicate fair skin. Another striking couple rolled by in a high-perched phaeton, and how that gentleman stared at his fair lady brought a hitch to her throat. Another lady walked a very small but fluffy dog on a leash, and a further lady, dressed in a serviceable gown walked with finely dressed twin girls toward the small park in front of the row of townhouses.

With each person she noticed, the piercing ache in her heart grew deeper and more biting. She had to admit to herself that it was far more than her first kiss that she yearned for. That thought made her shiver, and she wanted it to be proven untrue.

"It is for living," she said, closing her eyes briefly.

Dear Papa had always encouraged his girls to live a life of strict chaste restrictions and absolute moral correctness. Victoria had been so desperate to leave she had taken the risk to travel far away. Many in Biddleton had openly discussed how scandalous it had been for a vicar's daughter to travel without a husband. Her father had been censured for allowing her to behave so recklessly and so brazenly. The risk to her reputation and virtue had made Papa often seem utterly disappointed in his eldest daughter's choice. Marianne wished instead he could have celebrated her bravery in seeking a life of her own, untrammeled by prurient morality and stifling social expectations.

It suddenly struck Marianne how much she had prevented herself from experiencing, for fear of Papa's discontent.

She had been living each moment for her family and their rigid expectations, with little regard for the desires she owned in her heart. Her father wanted her to marry Dr. Grant, it had been evident in his every word and eager stare, whenever they had met. Marianne had known the doctor for over four years, and never once had she wondered what it would be like to press her lips against his own. It was because of that unrequited hope that Papa had resisted so hard and long against her determination to take up a post as a governess. She had hated refusing to submit to her father's fervent desire to see her marry the doctor, but she knew she would never be happy married to him. Fierce emotions tumbled through her, and she closed her eyes to trap her tears. Papa had always praised her for being his most sensible and levelheaded daughter. And that had encouraged her to bury the whimsy in her heart, but one strand of rebellion had resisted encouraging the doctor, who had made his desire to marry her quite clear.

> *I want more from life, Papa, and I am willing to find out exactly what I want and to pursue it. Whether I am to be a doctor's wife, a governess, a spinster, a world traveler, or a woman daring enough to accept her first kiss, I will discover it.*

For a moment she could hear only the pounding of her own heart, then she laughed, a weight of that overpowering burden unexpectedly lifting from her slender shoulders. *But I shan't be foolish*, she reminded herself staunchly. Especially when it came to musings of a gentleman with a certain crooked smile and a sensually slanted and a very kissable mouth. She especially must be sensible with him.

On this particular Friday night, Michael departed the club early, trusting the management for the night, especially the fighting pits, to Dorian Martin. There was a deep restlessness urging him to return home, and instead of withdrawing from the need, he followed it. At about two in the morning, he pushed a key in the heavy oak door and opened it.

The distant chime of music reached his ears, and he paused, soaking the delightful sound into his soul. He followed the powerfully haunting sound to the music room, where the door was slightly ajar. Michael slipped inside soundlessly and padded over to the girl seated before the pianoforte. Miss Ashbrook's eyes were closed, her brows furrowed in deep concentration, spikes of tears on her lashes as she played. He stood, in awe of her talent. Her fingers moved with passionate skill and grace, as she played an exquisite sonata by Pleyel.

Miss Ashbrook was simply impressive.

He stood behind her, not daring to make a sound lest he interrupted the magic flowing from her fingers. Several minutes passed before the delightful sounds petered away, and the tension seeped from her shoulders.

"Why did you not inform me, your lordship, that it is your brother Lord Thomas who is Lizzie's father?" she murmured without turning around.

"Thomas was here?" he said mildly, moving to sit beside her on the large bench.

"He was. Several hours earlier."

"I believe I mentioned that I was not Lizzie's father at our first meeting."

"I clearly did not believe you," she said with a soft side. "Please forgive me for not considering your claim."

He glided his fingers over the keys of the pianoforte. "Your sister believed my brother to be Lord Worsley. He foolishly wanted to impress her with a title."

"And Lucy would have been impressed with it."

He cast her a sidelong, measuring glance. There was deep sorrow in her tone, and he realized how painful it must be for her to witness her sister's fall from grace. The consequences of passion could be very severe for a young girl with little in the way of powerful connections.

"I am sorry," he said gruffly.

He felt her surprise.

"You are not responsible. And I…I received Lucy's letter this morning." She cleared her throat, delicately. "Thank you for your settlement. It will help her in deciding her future."

Michael sat down on the long bench beside her and started playing a lively glee. He was not sure what prompted him. Miss Ashbrook did not hesitate but joined him, and for several minutes, only the sound of their music swirled in the room. The music came to a sudden halt, and he shifted to see her staring at him. There was an awareness in her eyes which had not been present yesterday. This was new, something had changed, and his heart reacted with a harsh pound.

Her gaze dropped to his mouth for the briefest instant before she looked away quickly.

Dear God, she wanted to kiss him. He fisted his hands above the keys, creating a discordant sound, fighting to resist the sudden, astonishingly fierce urge to touch her face, to draw her against his body, to kiss her without consequences. He leaned close enough to breathe deeply of her, but keeping a respectable distance.

Think, damn it. Say something…anything. "Your playing is mesmerizing," he said gruffly.

A delighted smile crossed her lips. "Thank you, my lord."

More than anything, he wanted her to call him Michael. "Your governess taught you?"

"My mother was my music master," she murmured, her fingers dancing even faster of the keys, creating a sweet yet haunting melody. "I would practice several hours into the wee hours of the morning before the household woke. In Biddleton, I am often asked to play at our neighbors' country balls, and even at the larger assembly dances. I enjoyed playing of course, but not always for the entire night," she said with a light laugh. "Sometimes, I feel inspired to dance, but alas."

How wistful she sounded. "Ah…so you never dance."

"When I was a debutante, most certainly, but not in recent years." As if uncomfortable she had confessed such a thing, she sent him an overly bright smile. "You play beautifully, as well."

"In that, we have something in common. My mother taught me. My father never believed his sons should learn to play a musical instrument. I had a keen interest, so she happily taught me what she knew in secret."

"In secret!"

"My father had a rigid adherence of what he believed were pure masculine interests and what his sons should be taught," he said, surprised he had revealed so much of himself to her. With a disconcerted frown, he realized that he'd never had such a simple but complex conversation with any female of his past acquaintanceship.

"Is…is your mother still alive?" she asked tentatively.

"She is," he said with a chuckle. "She has been traveling for the last several years with her lady friend and companion and is now in Morocco. Her last letter implied she might return home soon."

"How long has she been traveling."

An odd pain twisted in his heart. "Almost nine years."

Her fingers faltered from the keyboard. "Upon my soul! That is an astonishingly long time to be away from home."

At his silence, she hurriedly added, "Please forgive me for prying."

How different she was from the other ladies in the *haut ton* who would have sensed a story they could gossip about and would have delicately started to pry. *How interesting you are, Miss Ashbrook.*

"My father killed himself," he found himself replying. "And after mourning for a few months, mother found the gossiping and the ceaseless speculating too much to bear. She fled…and I did nothing to stop her. I had desperately wanted to follow her to escape the responsibilities of an impoverished estate which had been unexpectedly dumped on my shoulders."

That was the first in ten years he had ever admitted that weakness to another soul. The discomfort of the awareness had him standing and moving away from the pianoforte. "I will bid you a pleasant night, Miss Ashbrook." And he walked away.

"Your lordship…"

He paused at the door and turned to face her. Her unbound hair rippled in wondrous waves down her back and over the front of her threadbare nightgown. It hid her figure completely, but that denial of flesh only tempted his baser urges more. What would it reveal should he take her in his arms, and remove that hideous garment? Lush curves, and luscious rounded hips, sweetly curved thighs that would welcome his weight atop her?

Repressing such thoughts, he allowed his gaze to remain only on her face. He huffed out a breath, not quite a laugh. That made no difference. Her loveliness was heart-jerking.

"I'll not betray the confidence you just shared with me," she said softly, her green eyes large and a bit pleading.

She didn't want him to go. His gut tightened in a rush of anticipation. But he must, for both their sakes. "I never thought you would, Miss Ashbrook."

Then he walked away and closed the door gently.

Good God. How much longer could he resist the temptation of her?

CHAPTER 8

A party of seven close friends lounged in Michael's drawing-room the following week. He'd hosted a private dinner which had finished some two hours' ago, and everyone had withdrawn to the drawing-room for some card playing, and general conversation. Wine, brandy, and port flowed freely, and no-one observed any rigid adherence that they must not drink or smoke in the presence of ladies. Michael thought with some amusement that all his friends were considered somewhat scandalous by the biddies of the *ton*.

At his home was his good friend, James, the Earl of Maschelly and his wife, Verity. Scandal had followed the couple several months' ago after James had taken her to the club, where disguised as a lad she had soundly defeated a blackguard who had hurt her in the past. Society had spoken of little else for weeks, but they were not hurt for it, for James and his countess hardly gave a damn what the *ton* thought of their wildly improper behavior. The only thing that had mattered to the earl was the newssheet had called her 'brave, daring, a society darling.' Michael also noted the slight bump below her alluring dark green silken evening gown, the sparkle in her brown eyes, and the tender way James would brush his hand along her hips and linger in a comforting caress. The glow of future motherhood enveloped her and was poignant for him to observe how proud Maschelly was of his lovely wife.

Present was also William, the Duke of Wycliffe, another of his friends who had been frequently mentioned in the scandal sheets a couple of weeks' past. One week the newspapers announced he was engaged to Lady Miranda who now sat before the pianoforte playing a lively tune with her husband, Dr. Simon Astor. The following week the scandal sheets could only talk about the duke having been jilted by Lady Miranda and informing the world he was busy chasing one Sophia Knightly publicly away from a ball, and yet now that lady was his duchess.

All three ladies were astounding beauties, and their unions were celebrated love matches. The last of his friends who was present was the only other unmarried person—Mr. Percy Taylor, a shrewd businessman who had been making waves with his housing ventures. The man believed in creating affordable homes for the lower classes, ones with sufficient space and hygienic sewage disposal. Michael had invested heavily with Percy and had no cause to regret it. There was a dark rumor going about that he was having an affair with a young countess who *was* still married to her seventy-year-old husband, but Michael had not pried into the man's private life, it was none of his business.

What a tangled web of scandal his closest friends had woven within society and Michael was one of the few who had never admonished them for their boldness. Of course, he himself stood on the brink of society's acceptance for his disreputable behavior.

"I heard the grounds have been broken on that new hospital you are building in your town," he said to Simon.

"It has. The building will commence next week, and Miranda is planning a charity fundraising ball for next month."

"I shall certainly be there with a sizeable contribution."

Simon smiled and lifted his glass of brandy in a toast.

"And how is business at the club," Maschelly asked, joining the conversation. "There is a great call for reform of gambling dens. I daresay it might affect your business endeavors in the future."

"Talking about business or politics must not happen tonight," the duchess cried from where she reposed in the chaise longue by the fire. "We need music and dancing. I daresay we should have hired a musician for our little gathering. I have the most pressing urge to dance with my duke." Then she winked.

Suddenly he was inspired, enough to say, "I do have the most talented player staying here."

That got all of his friends' attention.

"You have a musician under your roof? Why was the man not at dinner?" Percy asked with an arch of his brow.

"Miss Ashbrook…works for me."

"A servant who plays the pianoforte," Percy asked all astonished.

"She is a governess," he said cautiously.

"A governess!" Verity, Sophia, and Miranda chorused. "There is a child here?"

He stood, went over to the table with decanters of liquor, and poured himself a drink. "A baby of almost five months. Her name is Elizabeth…but we call her Lizzie. She is beautiful," he said. "Very even-tempered."

The silence was most profound. He glanced up to find Wycliffe staring at him. "You have a child?"

He felt a strange catch in his heart, and it befuddled Michael that it almost felt like regret. "No…she is not mine. When I am able to, I will share the circumstances of Lizzie's birth," he said gruffly.

Though several pairs of eyes glowed with curiosity, none pressed for more information. And he appreciated that about his friends.

"Miss Ashbrook is the most talented player of the pianoforte. I could ask her to play for us."

"Oh do," Lady Miranda cried and clapped. "We would all like that."

Michael summoned a maid who went to fetch Miss Ashbrook. A few minutes later, she knocked on the drawing-room door and entered. She faltered to see so many people staring at her, but lifted her chin, dipped into a most elegant curtsy. Though dressed in a simple dark gray serviceable gown, and her hair caught in a loose chignon with midnight black tendrils kissing her cheeks, Miss Ashbrook glowed with a radiant loveliness. Her green eyes stood out in a startling contrast against her pale skin.

"By Jove, she is most beautiful," Percy said, after a sharp intake of breath.

An oddly protective urge stirred inside Michael. "She is…and very much under my protection so direct your interest elsewhere."

The man sent him a probing glance. "Is she your mistress—"

"No," he said with more sharpness than he intended. "Simply an employee."

Michael stepped forward and made swift introductions. "May I present Miss Marianne Ashbrook," he said to no-one in particular. "Miss Ashbrook, my friends, the duke, and duchess of Wycliffe, the earl, and countess of

Maschelly, Dr. Simon Astor and his wife, Lady Miranda, and Mr. Percy Taylor."

She dipped into another deep and graceful curtsey, while smoothing nonexistent wrinkles from her dress. A flash of uncertainty crossed her features, which he was sure he only caught because of how keen he'd observed her every day since their first meeting. "I am very pleased to make your acquaintances."

"Lord Worsley has complimented your wonderful skills at the pianoforte. We do hope you could play some music for us to dance," the countess said with a wide, welcoming smile.

Miss Ashbrook sent him a surprised glance, and he faced her, blocking his friends' view of their interaction.

"I do hope I did not overstep," he murmured, noting her unexpected shyness.

"I have never played for such a grand audience before!"

He had taken her hand in his, and he could feel how wildly her pulse was fluttering. At her scandalized stare, he lowered her hand, hoping his friends had not seen his lapse in conduct. But from their very assessing and interested stares, they had noticed, and he acknowledged the fault. Shifting his regard back to Miss Ashbrook, it amused him to see she was biting her pretty lips and her cheeks were flushed.

"Do you feel unequal to the task?" he asked with some amusement.

She caught his eye and threw him a look so saucy and full of challenges that he nearly laughed out loud.

"Very well then," he said, stepping back.

She made her way over to the bench and sat, running her hand over the keys in a quick flourish of melody. Everyone hurriedly moved the table from the center of the room and pushed back a few of the sofas and the chaise longue for enough space to spin in the lively reel.

Miss Ashbrook did not disappoint, and soon Simon partnered his wife, and Verity was in James's arms dancing and laughing with each other.

Miss Ashbrook glanced toward the excited couples, and she too laughed, as if it was her on the makeshift dance floor. She had the most sensuous mouth he'd ever seen on a woman. Another glance at her sensual lips caused his cock to jump and harden. He glanced away quickly from that smiling mouth into the amused gaze of Wycliffe.

"I've never seen a lady captivate you so, you, my dear friend, you cannot stop staring. And I daresay from the quick glances Miss Ashbrook shoots your way she is equally transfixed," the duke said, taking a drink of his brandy.

Michael scowled. His preoccupation with Miss Ashbrook was becoming too noticeable.

"There is no enthrallment," he said a bit icily.

"Then why is there a rumor that for the last few months, you have been kicking out all the beauties sneaking into your private apartments at the club, without bedding them. And the last few society balls you attended you danced with no-one. People are taking notice that one of the *ton's* wickedest rakes is very distracted." The duke sent an assessing stare to Miss Ashbrook. "I believe I have discovered your distraction."

Michael knocked back his drink, the brandy burning a fiery trail to settle in his stomach. "Nonsense," he clipped. "I have been bored with it all long before I met Miss Ashbrook."

"But something about her does lighten the loneliness, doesn't it?" Wycliffe said, staring at his duchess.

Michael made no reply and shifted his regard to Percy,

who was no better in his avid watching of Miss Ashbrook with an air of rakish contemplation. Biting back the savage curse building inside, Michael decided to visit the club, needing the distraction from thinking about Miss Ashbrook's charms.

It was all damned ridiculous how many mornings he had lain abed with thoughts of taking her as his lover haunting his sleep and keeping him awake. He would not suffer it tonight. He would go to his gambling den and exhaust himself in the fighting pits.

And maybe then, he would sleep deeply at last without images of her muddling his mind and the tenuous hold he still had left on his honor.

ALMOST TWO HOURS after the viscount had summoned her to the drawing-room to meet his friends, they readied to depart. Marianne had never thought she would feel such ease of comfort in the presence of a duke and duchess. But the viscount's friends were charming and made every effort to welcome her. There had been no pretentious airs or displayed arrogance, and they had charmed her with their open welcome.

"Dear Miss Ashbrook," the duchess said with a wide smile. "How wonderful is your playing! Why, I've never heard anything equal to it. Thank you for obliging us in stealing your evening away."

Marianne smiled warmly at the beautiful and vivacious duchess. "Thank you, Your Grace. This was infinitely more enjoyable than the book I was reading." *Though only slightly!*

"Pish! Please call me, Sophia. I daresay we shall be close friends."

"I would like that, Sophia," Marianne replied, the familiarity feeling more natural than she'd expected.

The countess rounded Sophia and enfolded Marianne in a hug. "It was wonderful meeting you, Marianne, I do hope we meet again."

She murmured something noncommittal, not certain when she would ever get the chance to socialize with these people again.

Lady Miranda, a stunning beauty, clasped her hands. "Thank you for your lively music! I've not danced or laughed so much in a very long time."

"Oh, I have the very thing!" Sophia cried. "My very first ball as the Duchess of Wycliffe is next week. I would be so very pleased, Marianne, if you would attend."

Shock stole her breath for several minutes. Her at a duchess's ball? "I…forgive me, Sophia, but I couldn't!"

Her eyes sought out the viscount to see that he was staring at her, even though he conversed with the gentlemen. *Shameless!* With a flush, she looked away and noticed the speculative looks of the ladies as their gazes volleyed between them. She was mortified! No doubt they believed something improper was happening between the viscount and his governess.

"I know you might be worried about a suitable ball gown," Verity said, understanding gleaming in her eyes. "Since I do hope we might be dear friends; would you allow me to send around a gown that can no longer fit me?" Then she settled a hand on the gentle swell of her stomach as by way of explanation of why it no longer fitted her.

Embarrassment heated Marianne's cheek. She was not of their world, nor did she want their charity. She did note there was no pity in their expressions, and they genuinely seemed to like her.

"I will provide whatever gown Miss Ashbrook requires," a low voice drawled from behind her.

Marianne's eyes widened in horror at his lack of delicacy. She whirled to face him. "You will do no such thing," she said in scandalized dismay. Surely his assurances just now would imply she was his mistress.

An indecipherable emotion passed over his face. "I am your employer; it is my duty to take care of your needs. And I do believe I recall you mentioning you had not danced in ages."

Despite the thrum of excitement sliding through her veins, Marianne dismissed his words and faced the countess. "I do thank you, Lady Maschelly, for the kind offer. I…I will think about it and send word to your address of my decision."

Very conscious of how red her face and the tips of her ears must be, she dipped into a curtsy and bid everyone a good night, before fleeing the drawing room. Once in the hallway, she leaned against the oak-paneled wall. That wretched man! Surely, he knew what his possessive airs had implied. And why did her heart raced in such a manner to realize that he still wanted her? She drew a deep breath, trying to calm the wild pounding of her heart.

"She is so very lovely," the duchess said. "Is she your mistress?"

Marianne jerked from the wall, a hand fluttering to her mouth at that very blunt and intrusive question.

"Sophia," Lady Miranda admonished. "I can tell that Marianne is a lady of quality and sound judgment. She would not yield to his wicked wiles."

"How it heartens me to know my friends believe I could seduce an employee in my own household," came the viscount's dry and sarcastic reply.

"We have seen the look in your eyes, Michael," the duke said, apparently joining their improper conversation.

"That does not mean I would act on those blasted desires," he retorted. "Now let's discuss something else. I am off to the club, let me know if you will join me."

"Oh, I have always wanted to visit your club," breathed Lady Miranda. "Oh, do say we might attend, Simon!"

Marianne walked away and missed her husband's reply.

The viscount wanted her…his friends knew it…and the reason he had not been wicked with her was that she was a dependent in his household. At the top of the stairs, she paused and peered down in the darkened hallway. He was there, standing in the pocket of darkness, staring at her. Heat darted through her body, and her heart quickened. She could feel his stare, way down inside of her heart, and mystifyingly a deep ache unfurled through her. He had honor, and he might never kiss her in the way she often dreamed of.

The pang of disappointment was acute, yet such tenderness stirred in her heart. "Goodnight, your lordship," she said, staring in the darkness.

A few seconds passed, and then his low murmur floated to her.

"A pleasant rest to you, Miss Ashbrook."

CHAPTER 9

The sky hung dark overhead, the clouds a deep blue gray that threatened rain. Thunder rumbled ominously, and a fork of lightning cut across the sky, jerking Michael's gaze to the windows in his study. He slowly closed the ledgers the steward managing his ancestral seat in Derbyshire had sent over. The new farming equipment had improved the lives of his tenants significantly, and the repairs to the eastern section of the park wall surrounding Whittlestone Park had been fully completed. He hadn't been home in many years, choosing to stay in town even when the season had ended. It would be good to take Lizzie to the country, where he was certain Miss Ashbrook would enjoy taking long walks and picnics with her. Perhaps he could even join them on a few outings. It would also be good to remove them from the speculation he could already feel brewing in the *ton*.

Last night, another good friend of his, Sebastian, Viscount Shaw had mentioned that he heard Michael had stationed a mistress in his home. Michael had corrected him but hadn't liked the idea that people were indeed speculating about Miss Ashbrook's place in his life. No doubt there would soon be whispers as to the identity of the child she pushed daily in the perambulator.

A soft misting rain began to fall, and he glanced at the clock on the mantle. It was a little after ten in the morning. It was early yet, and sometimes Miss Ashbrook would still be out with Lizzie on a walk. With a curse, he hurried from the room and bounded up the stairs to the nursery. He opened the door to find Doris sitting by the windows with a softly cooing Lizzie snuggled in her arms.

The nursemaid paused in her storytelling and glanced up with a smile. "If you are looking for Miss Ashbrook, she has not yet returned from her walk, your lordship."

Michael nodded his thanks and returned downstairs where he called for the carriage. On impulse, he also collected a large umbrella, and a few minutes later, he was seated in the carriage, peering out the curtains. He had also informed the coachman to be on the lookout for her. Several minutes later, he spied her walking down the street, at times lifting her face to the rain. She was wet, her hat sat askew on her head, but there was a smile on her face. A cursory inspection showed the streets to be empty. He rapped on the roof of the carriage, and they slowed. Without waiting for the steps to be knocked down, he jumped from the equipage. She noticed him, and faltered, her lips forming a radiant smile.

He made his way over to her, opening the large umbrella as he drew closer. She moved closer to him so that she was sheltered.

"Oh, thank you, this is very unexpected but welcomed! I feared I would be a drowned rat by the time I arrived home."

Home. He truly liked that word coming from her and that she would think to call his townhouse home. "Would you like to take the carriage…or would you prefer to keep walking?"

Michael wasn't sure what madness had just seized him, but he was glad it had, for she dealt him a most radiant smile.

"I would like to continue walking."

The sky chose that moment to dump torrents of rain on the streets. Peering at the sleeting rain, her expression became crestfallen. With a sigh, she stepped toward the parked carriage, and he halted her. She became aware of the clasp on her wrist and tried to draw her hand away.

He moved slightly back, breaking the contact. "If you would place your hand on my arm, Miss Ashbrook, we will continue with our stroll."

Thick lashes framed her extraordinary green eyes, which glowed with bold curiosity as she peered up at him. "We will?"

"Most certainly."

"In the rain? It is at least a twenty minutes' walk."

"Why not be whimsical?"

"I quite like the sound of that," she said with a light laugh and delight in her gaze.

And they walked side by side, the umbrella a small protection from the slanted rain. The coachman who would no doubt be exceedingly puzzled drove the carriage at a snail's pace behind them.

She cast him a quick sidelong glance. "Might I enquire, your lordship, as to why you own a club? It is something I have been most curious about. I do not think it common for a man of your stature to own a gambling establishment with a rumored fighting den as well!"

"My father…he died when I was only twenty leaving the estates in bad need of funds. Creditors were also knocking, and I had my brother, who was only thirteen at the time and a grief-stricken mother to provide for."

"Oh, how terrible," she said, her voice soft with sympathy.

And suddenly he did not want to whitewash what had happened. "My father gambled and lost his fortune, several hundred acres of lands, and a couple of unentailed estates. When he realized the severity of it, he made his way home and killed himself. I tried to shield my mother and brother from the brunt of the scandal and did everything in my power to protect them from a life of poverty. That included selling all our notable paintings, the silverware, and anything of value I could get my hands on. I invested in a gambling hell…and a year later our fortunes started to change."

She went utterly still, and he had little choice but to stop walking. When he peered down at her, her eyes were wide with such sadness and compassion.

"And it is that pain your mother has lived through for the last several years. Oh, I am so terribly sorry." Unexpectedly she lifted a hand and cupped his jaw.

Michael sucked in a harsh breath. Her soft caress, so light it was scarcely a breath of sensation, pierced him like a well-aimed arrow. This was the first time she had voluntarily touched him, and he felt like someone had handed him the keys to a kingdom.

The rain beat a wild rhythm on the surface of the umbrella, a gust of wind blew in the droplets to wet their faces and clothes, yet neither moved. Tendrils of water ran from the brim of her hat onto her cheeks, and it was his turn to use his thumb to wipe away the trail.

Michael tucked a strand of wet hair behind her ear, his knuckle barely grazing her cheek. The feel of her skin was soft and so supple. "I do not deserve your compassion after the pain my family has caused yours," he said gruffly.

Her eyes darkened, and her gaze lowered to his mouth momentarily, before she lifted her eyes to his. "I'll not blame you for the action of another."

Yet he saw the pain and shame in her eyes as if her sister's ruination reflected on herself.

"And you are not to blame for your sister's actions."

Miss Ashbrook blinked up at him, visibly shocked. She lowered her hand, and he felt bereft. *Touch me again*, he wanted to implore, but he remained silent.

"I knew there was someone she liked," she said so softly, he almost did not hear her above the rumble of rain. "We exchanged letters often, and I sensed the ruination in every sentence as she spoke about the most handsome and amiable gentleman she had ever met. And I did nothing to stop her fall from grace."

She swallowed, looked away, and continued walking. They moved in silence, their steps in tune with each other, perhaps each contemplating their siblings.

She glanced at him sidelong. "I am not silly or vain enough to wallow in self-pity and blame by thinking I had the power to control Lucy's heart or her actions. She has always been very willful and would rush headlong into trouble heedless of my warnings. But I am very saddened that she was hurt, and there are days I wish I could take the pain away for her."

"That I understand," he murmured, for he felt the same about Thomas.

They strolled closely together for another few minutes, the wind whipping the droplets in their faces. Each time he thought to suggest they board the carriage, he only had to look down and see the contentment showing on her face and swallowed down his words. He thought of the upcoming ball and how delighted she had appeared at the invitation. Michael did not mention that he had also requested of the countess an invitation for her to another ball a few weeks from now.

"Will you save two dances for me?"

She met his eyes, her gaze startlingly direct. "At the ball?"

"Where else would we dance?" he asked with amusement wafting through him.

She shocked him silly by rushing from under the umbrella and doing a perfectly elegant and charming pirouette in the rain. Within seconds she was soaked, and she removed her hat and tilted her face to the sky. When she lowered her head, there was such mischief and a wicked invitation in her eyes, he lost the ability to breathe. Did she not realize how provocative and alluring she appeared? The dark blue service dress now seemed like a gift wrapper, waiting for him to carefully peel back the layers and undo the most delicious present.

"We could dance in the rain!" she cried, laughing. "Oh dear, have *I* done something that shocked Viscount Wicked? I must say I am impressed with myself."

She seemed so…*alive*. That weird malaise which had gripped him for so long suffered its first crack, and a curious sensation fluttered in his chest. He glanced up and down the street, noting that it was empty of carriages. Lifting his head, he indicated for his coachman to carry on and not wait for them. The man obeyed, and Michael tugged her to his side under the shelter of the umbrella and waited for the coach to pass them.

Then he encircled her waist with one hand, while holding the umbrella firmly with the other, and with ridiculous ease twirled her with several movements of the waltz.

"Oh! Are you to join me?"

"It seems your lunacy is catching."

She followed his lead, and anyone who saw them dancing in the rain with an umbrella above them like loons would surely believe they had recently escaped from Bedlam.

"This is glorious," she said, laughing.

"You'll not say that when you are sneezing, shivering abed with a cold and fever," he warned.

"Oh, I have the sturdiest constitution. Many times, in Biddleton on my long walks, I've been caught in a downpour." The laugh fell away from her lips, and the hands clasping his shoulders suddenly went stiff. "And this is also very *improper*." Her lips were trembling.

He stared at her a moment, trying to gather his wits. "I doubt there can be anything truly improper between friends."

Her breath caught audibly. She stepped away from him, and he released her. Wide eyes searched his face, then she said, "Is that what we are…friends, your lordship?"

"We are more than employee and employer. I daresay friend is the apt term."

She gave him a smile of such breath-taking sweetness, he wondered for the first time in his life, if a part of falling in love was akin to the sensation of warmth and hunger suffusing throughout his entire body.

He felt oddly unnerved. Michael did not like the sensations coursing through him one bit, they felt foreign, not a part of him or something he could control. The very idea that he could not repress the sudden pounding of his heart or the heat in his body or the urge to laugh was intolerable.

"You are frowning," she said tenderly. "Most severely too."

Then she lifted a hand and touched the corner of his mouth. "I have meant to ask about this cut."

"I've been fighting," he said gruffly. "At the club these past couples of nights."

"Why?"

To forget this awful need clawing in my gut for you.

"Sometimes I do," he said instead. "Then I donate my winnings to charity."

"Admirable, and perhaps worth a bruise or two."

"Come, let's hurry. I can tell the deluge will worsen."

She gasped audibly when their fingers lightly brushed. And he understood, for he savored that fleeting caress. "Tell me about yourself, Miss Ashbrook," he invited, quite hungry to know all the facets of the woman walking beside him.

She wrinkled her nose. "As my sisters often complain, I am frightfully boring. Let me see. I have an incurable sweet tooth. I love reading, and Papa has long given up on my poor reading choices. I adore gothic romances."

"So do I."

"I suppose you identify with the villain in those pieces."

He would not dignify that with a response.

Her smile was barely perceptible. "I do have a confession. Many times, I wish the heroines would fall in love with that brooding, dastardly villain! But I am always disappointed it isn't so."

"Ah…so you like villains, do you?"

"I *am* walking with you now in the rain and living with you under your roof."

He allowed himself a brief, hungry study of her animated features. "So, you like me?"

"Tolerably enough."

Despite the dreariness of the afternoon, she was a slice of sunlight walking beside him.

"At first, I deplored the thought of being a governess. I was eager to retain a measure of independence, so I responded to Lord Sanderson's advertisement."

"Why did you not want to become a governess?"

"I love children, but there is nothing mildly exciting about such a post," she said primly. "In Jane Austen's *Emma*, she said 'to become a governess is to retire from all pleasures of life!' I daresay such a notion filled me with dread. But I resolved such a post must only be temporary. I often have dreamed of adventures which might be ordinary to a man of your experience and wealth."

"Such as?"

"Traveling beyond the town of Biddleton..., since I read Victor Hugo's *Notre-Dame de Paris*, I've wanted to desperately see the Notre-Dame Cathedral. Perhaps even the Château de Versailles. I also think it would be grand to purchase any number of books I desire without worrying about the cost, dressing in fine silks, dancing the night away," she admitted with a self-conscious smile.

Something tender and shockingly vulnerable settled on her face. "But beyond those...I...I desire a family of my own."

Those softly spoken words were a brutal kick to his gut. A family of her own...that meant a husband, someone else kissing her, making love with her, dancing in the rain with her...and bringing forth that smile that could rival the heat and beauty of the sun.

"We are at your home," she said with a shaky laugh. "And we are two drowned rats."

With that simple smile and anxious eyes, she knocked the breath from him. At his lack of response, her smile faded, her eyes darkened with nameless emotions. Miss Ashbrook twirled around and rushed up the small steps. As if the butler had been peeking out, the door opened, and she disappeared over the threshold. The door remained open, but Michael only gripped the handle of the umbrella a bit tighter and continued walking. It felt like he was running from something, but he was not entirely sure what truth he hoped to disavow.

CHAPTER 10

A few days later, the morning of the ball arrived, and Marianne was much preoccupied with the duchess's invitation. Of course, she could not attend the ball. There was nothing in her valise that would be suited for a simple soirée much less a midnight ball given by a duchess! Nor did she feel comfortable with wearing a dress which belonged to Lady Maschelly. But such a longing resided in Marianne's heart to go. On a deep breath, she pushed through her disappointment. She would procure her address from the viscount and send a polite letter thanking her for the wonderful invite but declining.

With that firm decision made, she'd proceeded with her morning by taking her niece on their daily walk, which was cut once again short by the rumble of thunder. The dreary weather had not lowered her spirit, it had served as a delightful reminder of her interlude in the rain with the viscount.

Something between them had changed that day, and to Marianne, it felt more than friendship. Friends should certainly not be awkward with each other. The viscount had been present at dinner last night, and the entire atmosphere had been filled with a perilous tension. How her heart had pounded and how uncertain she had felt… Marianne had hurried to her chambers afterward and had waited with dread and anticipation of the viscount knocking on her door. Never before had she had such a restless night.

With a befuddled sigh, she closed the children's storybook she was reading to Lizzie. Marianne spent the rest of the day reading and writing letters to her sister Lucy in Bath, one to Victoria in Brussels, and to her Mama and Papa in Biddleton.

When the dinner bell sounded, she requested a tray to be sent to her room and ate the delicious fare of roasted duck, asparagus in crème sauce, tender slices of roasted pork, with roasted potatoes and a delicate cream sauce flavored with dill. With each bite she'd wondered if the viscount sat eating alone or if he had made his way to the club, or to the duchess's ball. Having her fill, she set the tray outside and sat on the comfortable ledge seat by her room's window.

From her view, a little of the cobbled street could be seen, and she watched a line of carriages rolling by, a wistful yearning filled her heart. A knock sounded, and she glanced over her shoulder. A young maid entered and informed Marianne a few packages had been delivered for her. She made her way down the curving staircase. Stepping into the hallway, a footman held three boxes in his hands.

"These are for me?"

"Yes," he said with a pleasant smile. "There were just delivered, Miss."

Considerably astonished, she took the boxes, climbed the stairs, and made her way back to her room. She frowned upon seeing a note of sorts peeking from the largest box. Marianne collected the note and folded it open.

Dear Miss Ashbrook,

I gather you would be in most severe anxiety of what to wear at the Duchess's midnight ball. I've taken the liberty to use my connections with a particular modiste to order you a gown. Now, please remove that very fierce and fighting frown from your pretty face.

With a gasp, Marianne snapped her gaze to the mirror on her vanity. She *was* frowning. Biting her lip to prevent her laughter, she continued reading.

Three boxes should have been delivered. One with a gown, another with unmentionables, and another with such exquisite dancing slippers for a mad moment I thought to try them on myself. But regrettably, my feet were too big.

She was laughing. She couldn't help it. A soft sob escaped her, a deep breath shuddered from her, and she realized her eyes had welled. She was on the verge of crying like a silly goose. She couldn't help that, either. It was all so improper and shocking, and so wonderful.

I do hope I acquitted myself by making you laugh and how sorry I am to have missed it. Please accept this token of friendship and say yes to attending the ball.

Worsley.

Marianne dropped the note on the bed and opened the lid of the largest box. The most exquisite gown sat on a sheaf of delicate papers. She lifted the dress gingerly to her face, admiring the sheer richness of the material, and the exquisite cut and design.

Could she dare to wear such an improper gift from the viscount? She gently placed it back in its box and opened the other. Half white silk gloves and the most delicate silken stockings. A corset which clearly cost a pretty penny, a lace chemisette, and even pantalettes.

A knock sounded, and the young maid who had attended her so diligently, Harriet, entered the room.

"The viscount bid me to help you ready for the ball, Miss Ashbrook. The carriage will be ready in a couple hours. We should start," she said with a warm smile.

A soothing bath in rose-scented water did much to relax Marianne. The maid had assisted her in dressing and now styled her hair before the dressing table. With each curl and twist, she stared at herself, wondering at the young lady who stared back with wide excited eyes.

"This must be what Cinderella felt like," she said with a light laugh.

"Oh, Miss, you are ever so beautiful," Harriett said.

Marianne stood, staring at the picture she presented. This gown was the most luxurious thing she had ever worn and must have cost a frightful sum. It was a dark rose low-cut gown with its tightly cinched waist and wide skirt. It revealed more décolletage than she had ever shown before, but she felt exquisite.

Marianne looked…*pretty*. Remarkably so. Giddy delight washed through her, and she did a slight twirl before the mirror, before gathering her courage to step out into the hall. She straightened her back and ignored all her fears as she swept down the long staircase. Down below the viscount waited, staring up at her with a slight smile on his face.

She had never seen the viscount dressed in such an elegant manner. He'd donned dark trousers, a white shirt, with a waistcoat of pale blue watered silk, an expertly tied silken cravat, and a rich midnight-black swallow-tailed coat. Instead of cutting his overlong hair, it had been caught at his nape with a black velvet ribbon. How terribly handsome he appeared.

The viscount's eyes trailed down her body in a manner he had never allowed her to see before—a rude intimacy that made her spine stiffen and had her flushing. His beautiful dark silver-gray eyes glowed hotly, and about his lips was a sensual, almost cruel curve. Flames of unwanted desire twisted through Marianne, and she sucked in a harsh breath. Another never-before felt delicate tendril of heat spun through her body, and her heart shuddered in warning.

"I've met the gentleman, *and* the charmer," she murmured, a bit of wickedness stirring inside her, and returning his bold stare. "Am I to meet the rake tonight?"

His expression suddenly turned distinctly sensual. "And would you be receptive to the rake?"

A dark throb of indefinable emotions throbbed in his voice. It made her unaccountably wary. "I would be silly to…surely that would only lead to ruin and heartbreak."

Lord Worsley studied her with an odd gravity, then he said, "You are astoundingly ravishing, Miss Ashbrook."

That bit of awe in his soft murmur scattered her thoughts for a precious moment. "Thank you," she said simply, gliding her gloved hand across the elegant bannister of the staircase.

They walked down the hallway without speaking, and he went into the drawing-room, then reappeared with a stunning burgundy evening coat which complemented her evening gown. He assisted her into the coat, and she was so very conscious of the powerful, masculine frame behind her.

Soon they were in the carriage which rumbled toward the duchess's home in Grosvenor Square. He made no effort to introduce conversation, and Marianne realized that she felt incredibly nervous. "I suspect I will be the brunt of many curious stares, and probing questions."

"Perhaps. Simply ignore them. You'll be admired for your beauty and elusive quality."

Humor lit inside. "I quite like the sound of that." And she idly wondered when all of this would disappear, and she returned to her normal life. *Tonight is what I shall make it.*

A short while later, they arrived behind a long queue of carriages. She swiped aside the curtain on the carriage and peered outside. Several people were alighting from their equipages and walking the short distance to the townhouse. They were so splendidly garbed she gasped, admiring the elegance of the ladies and the aristocratic handsomeness of the gentlemen.

The viscount knocked on the roof of the carriage, and the steps to their coach were knocked down. He went out before her, held up his hand, and assisted her down.

"Miss Ashbrook," a feminine voice called.

She glanced up and spied Lady Maschelly. "Verity," she cried, truly delighted to see her. "How beautiful you are." The countess was indeed ravishing in a light blue tightly-waist gown with a delightful revealing décolletage. White satin elbow-length gloves encased her slender arms, and her golden dancing slippers gleamed. Her earl was equally dressed in the first stare of fashion in dark trousers and matching jacket, and a peach striped waistcoat. They made a handsome couple.

"Lord Maschelly," she greeted with a quick curtsy. "Lady—"

"None of that," the countess said. "We insist you call us James and Verity."

They went inside as a quartet, Marianne and Verity walking a bit forward with the gentlemen at the rear. Marianne could feel the viscount's eyes on her, the touch of his gaze as physical as a caress. She felt acutely aware of her own body and the way he made her heart ache. She equally resented and welcomed that fevered, desperate longing she had inside for him to touch her.

No good could ever come from longing for a rake!

They spent a few minutes in the receiving line, and she laughed and chatted with Verity with an ease that surprised Marianne. She was terribly excited to be at her first *ton* ball and tried her very best to mask her reactions. Laughter and chatter drifted around her, music floated all around them, and the scent of flowers—roses, jasmine, and lilacs were redolent on the air.

They were announced, and soon she was in the glittering world of an overflowing crush of a ballroom. Dozens of chandeliers created a dazzling display of light. The duchess approached in an exquisite golden gown, her dark brown hair with its golden highlights was piled high in a riot of curls. She greeted them gaily, a becoming pink blushing her face, her eyes alight with her own excitement. Every public space of the townhouse seemed to be overflowing with guests, and even beyond the wide-open windows, Marianne spied guests strolling in a garden festooned with hanging lanterns.

Her senses felt assaulted with such sweet mixtures of perfumed scents, the gay laughter, the clinking of champagne glasses, and the lovely music from the orchestra's bows.

The duchess introduced her to several people, and her family, one Aunt Imogen who was really the Countess

Cadenham, her cousins Lady Lydia, and Viscount Portman who quickly charmed her with artful flattery and requested a few dances.

Marianne happily nodded and danced a few sets, determined to enjoy an experience she doubted she would ever have again. Marianne was not in the habit of indulging ridiculous fancies, but tonight she would enjoy herself gloriously.

Almost two hours later, she finally found herself on the sidelines, drinking a very refreshing punch.

"Miss Ashbrook."

The bands she hadn't known were around her chest loosened. "My Lord Worsley," she murmured, as he made his way to stand beside her.

"I have it on the highest authority a waltz will be announced."

The dratted man said nothing else but stared at her with keen anticipation.

"Is that an invitation to dance, your lordship? Because it sadly lacks in charm."

The viscount moved to stand in front of her and bowed. "I would be forever delighted if you should honor me with this next dance."

"Why, after asking so prettily I must oblige."

A smile crept up into his eyes and lurked at the corners of his mouth. He was so beautiful, in a uniquely male way. He led her to the dance floor, and as the viscount swept her in his arms, she could feel the weighted speculation of everyone in the ballroom buzzing across her skin like insects. Especially the very naked lady she had spied that first day in the viscount's drawing-room.

"Everyone is staring," she whispered, unable to prevent her wide smile.

"Mostly, the gentlemen," he murmured. "They are all

wondering who is this beautiful creature in my arms and how they might get to know you."

"I suppose it would take another rake to know."

His lips curved as he turned her into an exciting glide. She didn't like his smile. It drew her eyes instantly to his mouth and made her think of debauchery and things a respectable woman should not wonder about.

What would your lips upon mine taste like? Though she had never been kissed, every feminine instinct warned her there would be a taste, an evocative one that would enrapture her senses. Marianne was unwillingly captivated, and she feared he saw it in her eyes.

They danced and chatted about inane things she would unlikely recall in the morning. The man was just as abreast with all the rumors of the *ton* as the most notorious gossip would ever be. He had thrilled her curious senses by informing her of the latest scandals, even ones he swore only he knew. How he had gleaned such information he hadn't revealed.

"And that is Lord Rawlings standing by the potted plant, brooding into his glass of champagne. It is said he is in love with his valet."

"How outrageous," she gasped, laughing as he twirled with her. "I am certain you made that up."

He winked. "Ah…but only a few know that his valet is actually an American heiress in hiding from her dastardly step-father. And he knows it."

He smiled down at her, and in his eyes, she spied a desire which mirrored her own. And her greatest fear and wonderment was…what would Viscount Wicked do about it?

CHAPTER 11

Almost an hour after dancing with his lordship, Marianne escaped through the open terrace doors into the gardens. The crowd was a frightful crush, and her very bones ached from all the dancing, laughing, and chatting.

It amazed her that ladies of the *haut monde* attended such lavish balls almost nightly. She passed a few couples who seemed as if they had slipped outside for illicit liaisons. She could hear the strains of music spilling through the doors from the ballroom, beckoning her to return, but her feet ached dreadfully. Moving in the opposite direction of a darkened section of the lantern-lit gardens, she tipped her face to the sky and laughed. "Tonight has been wonderful."

And if her Papa knew he would be sorely disappointed that she had been caught admiring such a lush and decadent lifestyle. *I must forge my own wants and opinions, Papa.* The sweetest ache stirred in her heart, and her throat ached from the memory of how she danced with Lord Worsley. How perfectly they had fitted together.

Oh, I must stop thinking of him!

The viscount was not likely to ever marry her, a young miss with no connections or fortune, and her silly heart would not stop yearning for the dratted man. She rounded a corner and almost collided with the duchess's cousin. Lady Lydia's face was flushed red, and her eyes glittered with some unknown emotions.

"Is all well, Lady Lydia?" Marianne inquired tentatively.

"Oh yes, but I would urge you to not visit *that* section of the gardens if you understand my meaning."

Marianne frown. "I do not…*oh*!" Lydia had caught someone in *flagrante delicto*. "How mortifying, I hope you were not seen."

Lady Lydia giggled. "It seems Viscount Wicked will be libertine wherever he goes, even if it is a duchess's ball."

"Viscount Worsley?"

She nodded, her soft golden curls bouncing against her rounded cheeks. "Why, yes, the very same! He has the most notorious reputation, you know."

"I see," she said, pressing a hand over her suddenly aching heart. The hot sting of tears burned her eyes.

"Despite his wicked reputation, he is *very* wealthy and one of the most elusive catches of the season. Just now he set the gossipmongers' tongues wagging by only dancing with—"

Lady Lydia gasped as recognition dawned in her eyes. "Oh, it was you he danced with!" she said, her voice soft with sympathy.

Marianne turned with as much dignity as she could muster not understanding why the evidence of his licentious manner should hurt in such an awful manner. *He is my employer*, she hardly berated herself. Yet her feet, as if they had a mind of their own, tugged her to that secluded section of the beautiful gardens.

"I do not think it wise for you—"

She scarcely heeded this, for her attention was claimed by the lady in the Viscount's arm. They appeared as if caught in a passionate embrace. The picture of him with another woman brought a twisting pain that filled her with too much confusion.

"Unhand me," the young lady cried. "I have exerted myself in every imaginable way to win your regard, and you continually ignore me!"

It was then Marianne noted he was actually trying to do up the lady's gown, not undress her. The relief which darted through her was so profound, she lifted trembling fingers to her lips.

The viscount had cloaked himself in a mask of civility. "If you ever throw yourself in my arms in such a manner again, you will feel my wrath," he snapped, pushing her away from him.

She stumbled, but he hardly seemed to care.

The lady's lips were pinched, fire spat from her eyes, and fury tautened her frame. "I will inform my father of this! Honor will demand that you marry me."

His soft, mocking laugh disconcerted Marianne.

"I am not interested in that state, Miss Benedict. If I were, I would have married years' ago."

Marianne flinched, the twinges in her heart shifting to a pounding ache.

Miss Benedict began tearfully, "After I tell my father how you've compromised me, he will insist—"

"How bloody naïve. Nothing could induce me to marry a spoiled, grasping brat such as yourself."

The lady lifted her hand to slap him, and he caught it in a punishing vice.

Marianne must have made some noise, for his head snapped toward her, and his expression shuttered. The lady tugged her hand from his and whirled around to see what had arrested his attention.

"I have a witness," she gasped dramatically. "Lord Worsley has compromised me!"

The viscount stepped around the lady and stared at Marianne.

"I thought it was *you*," he said softly.

A soft breath shuddered from her when he plucked a piece of paper from his top pocket and held it up.

"I thought the note to meet here was from you."

The lady's face mottled with anger. "How dare you think that creature better than me! She is a crass bore who does not belong in our world. I cannot imagine what the duchess thought by inviting her! I heard the whispers in the retiring room that she is posing in your home as a governess after birthing your bastard—"

"Do not dare?" Lord Worsley snapped low and dangerous. "I marvel that you should have the effrontery to call Miss Ashbrook's honor into question after your behavior. Another word…or breath in Miss Ashbrook's presence and I will ruin your father completely. I will call in his fifty thousand-pound debt to my club and have him blackballed. Every club he is a part of will cut him out, and I will ensure you are never invited to another ball or soirée. Such viperous spite deserves no less."

His calm ruthlessness shocked Marianne. The young lady burst into tears, her shoulders shaking, her bare breast quivering. Marianne stepped forward to help her. His lordship came toward her, grabbed her hand and tugged her from the alcove.

"She needs help to redress," Marianne said, trying to tug her hand from his.

"Leave her!"

She winced at the hard implacability in his tone.

Marianne tried again to reclaim her arm, his clasp tightened, and she abandoned the attempt, coloring faintly. "Your lordship…my lord…Michael!"

He stopped and dropped her hand. "The first time you say my name will not be to plead for that undeserving wretch!"

"Then when should I say it?" she snapped, quite irritated with his high-handed manner.

It flashed in his eyes so fast she almost missed it. Desire—potent and scalding. In his gaze, she saw kisses and tangled limbs atop twisted sheets. He wanted to make love to her, and *that* was when he wanted her to cry his name. Marianne trembled and his eyes sharpened. "You…you said you would never marry," she whispered, and then closed her eyes in abject mortification. "*Please*, do not answer. This conversation is highly improper and unnecessary." Marianne would die if he believed she was desperately hoping for marriage from him.

He nodded once and turned away. They exited the side gardens and made their way to the front of the bustling townhouse.

"We are not to say our farewells?"

"I will send a note of apology."

The carriage was called around, and she waited as he went inside and collected her coat. His lordship did not speak as he slipped it on. She valiantly fought her reaction when his fingers brushed along her nape.

It was impossible to think she could stay under the viscount's roof for long unless she learned to govern the reactions he evoked within her. Marianne didn't want to lose being with Lizzie, but it might be better for her heart and virtue if she took a post elsewhere and visited her niece on her off days.

The carriage came around, and he assisted her inside. Tonight, she had met the ruthless part of him that had allowed him to own and operate a gambling den and fight pits. To think that he could threaten to ruin Miss Benedict's father in such a cruel manner. And it scared her that perhaps he would in fact do so.

Her skin felt too tight, and she was painfully aware of how close he sat in the carriage. "Miss Benedict," she began haltingly. "She is very young and misguided."

"You are younger than her."

How cold and dismissive he sounded.

"I would still like you to forgive her rash and very stupid actions."

"No."

"My lord—"

"You did not deserve her attack, nor does she warrant your consideration."

"It is our Christian duty—"

A bark of harsh laughter cut her off. "You forget that I am wicked and unprincipled? Such arguments will not sway me."

"I would still like it if you would forgive her," she said quietly, folding her hands in her lap.

He stared at her for a long time. "I will forget about it this one time. Miss Benedict will not be let off lightly should she ever approach you again."

"Thank you. We are not of the same society. I doubt we will ever cross paths in the future. And I daresay after the scare you gave her, her willful ways might be improved."

His lips curled in a sardonic smile, but he made no

reply, simply shifting into the pockets of shadow in the carriage.

The rest of the journey was spent in silence, and Marianne did nothing to break the odd tension now between them. For she was distracted by a shattering awareness. If he had been making love with Miss Benedict, it would have hurt her most deeply. And he had no interest in marriage. That meant the wicked desire he stared at her with…if she should ever surrender, would mean her ruination. The knowledge settled like heavy stones against her chest, crushing and frightening.

CHAPTER 12

Michael closed the play he had been reading, a beautifully bound edition of *Othello*, and stood. Tonight, he had not gone to his club, finding that the deepening dissatisfaction in his heart had spread to encompass a distaste for his own gambling den. He laughed to himself over how he had tried to wipe out his feeling of ennui for his usual pastimes. Even the punishing bloody fights of the last few nights had filled him with no satisfaction. He had emerged the victor mostly unscathed, but he felt no pride at his achievements. It had not blotted out the ever-present mind-destroying lust that he acknowledged was driving through his blood. It disconcerted him to know his greatest source of pleasure now was Miss Ashbrook's smile.

How utterly ridiculous, bewildering, yet so fascinating. Something about her made him think about a family of his own. A daughter…a son…a wife. Marriage was something he would eventually do, even though he had never felt a pressing urge to contemplate the state. A few years' ago, tupping one woman for the rest of his life had seemed like the gravest of sins, a folly that he could resist.

But now…he hadn't a lover in so long, he wondered if he would know what to do with a lady should she lie before him and split her legs open.

His cock jerked when that image revealed Miss Ashbrook. With a savage curse, he shut it away from his thoughts. Since the night of the duchess's ball, they had been tiptoeing around each other. It amused and perplexed him in equal measures. Oftentimes he could feel her watching him, but whenever he looked her way, she would glance away quickly and study something else. For God's sake, earlier he had caught her studying the hothouse flowers in the hallway as if they would unlock the mysteries of the world.

Her reaction had filled him with humor, and something far more tender and elusive. Michael left his study and climbed the stairs. As he passed by the nursery, he heard crying. He frowned, for it was after eight and Lizzie would usually be sound asleep by this time.

He opened the door to find Doris pacing with her, but the child cried even louder.

"Your lordship," she said, looking a bit tired. "I am not certain what the problem is. She has been crying now for several minutes. I've fed her and changed her. But she is still fussing. I am certain I'll have her sleeping soon."

Yet the crying increased in volume. He made his way inside and held out his arms for her. Doris gently placed her in his arms, and he held her to his chest, murmuring soothing loving words of nonsense. It made no difference, her screams only got louder. Lizzie's obvious misery cut into him, he felt useless, being unable to pacify his niece. He looked down at her red, angry, crying face and realized with a thump how much the little girl had become part of his life. He hated seeing her this unhappy.

"Let me get Miss Ashbrook," he said, resting Lizzie in her softly padded cradle. Then he strolled down the hallway and knocked on Miss Ashbrook's door. No reply came, and with a frown he considered that she might be sleeping. Still, he opened the door and lost his ability to breathe.

She stood totally naked before her bed, singing softly and sweetly, as she dried the water droplets that sparkled on her body like diamonds under the firelight. He had never seen a female form that mouth-wateringly voluptuous, or one he wanted more. Midnight black hair rippled in glorious waves over her shoulders and back, falling below her waist. Most of that hair covered her breasts, but he greedily took in the smooth flatness of her stomach, those wide flaring hips, her curved thighs, and elegant legs. She turned, and he bit back a groan at the rounded curve of her delightful rump. Arousal burned through him in violent, astonishing waves, fierce and all-consuming, unlike anything he had ever felt before.

Michael gripped the doorknob and tried to gather his scattered wits. *Concentrate on the task at hand, you bloody bacon-brained idiot.* The savage curse did nothing to rouse him from the twisting needs humming through his body. And he knew then he had lost the fight. Perhaps once a rake always a rake. The wicked seducer in him stirred, and he would have her, under him, above, deeply sheathed on his cock; whichever way he wanted. And he wanted all of that and far more,

"Sweet Mercy."

A REVERENT WHISPER had Marianne's head snapping up. The viscount was framed by the doorway, his expression one of aroused greed. Shock stole her breath for precious seconds, then she yanked the large towel to her throat as if it would shield her from that predatory gaze.

"Your lordship!"

His gaze collided with hers and his hand fell away from the doorknob. A powerful heat flared in the depth of his gaze. She saw the evidence of his struggle and her heart jerked at the awareness of how much he desired her. A heady feeling rushed through her, a hot and delicious tingle low down in her body.

"It is Lizzie…she is crying and cannot be soothed. I thought…" he raked a hand over his hair, his expression cloaked in sensuality as if it were a second skin.

Wrapping the towel around her, she rushed toward him and slammed the door in his face.

"Dear God," she whispered, pressing her forehead against the cool surface of the door. Then she sprang into motion and hurried to where she had laid out her nightgown on the chaise longue by a window. Dropping the towel on the floor and uncaring that she had not fully patted dry her body, she drew on her nightgown, without adding a chemise.

She felt vulnerable being naked under the cotton material, but she could not think about that now. Without pushing her feet into slippers, she all but ran to the door, opened it and brushed past the viscount who was still standing there. She went into the nursery and took a screaming Lizzie from a very flustered Doris.

Upon seeing her, Lizzie calmed only slightly, a soft sob hiccupping from her. Marianne removed her niece's clothing and checked her over. There was a slight redness on one of her arms, and she supposed that it would sting a bit. "Perhaps an insect got in through the window and bit her," she said softly.

Doris hurried to the small desk in the room and withdrew a salve. Marianne rubbed it on that red spot, redressed Lizzie in her soft nightgown, and sat with her in the rocker by the window, gently singing to her. It took several minutes for her cries to lessen, then her lashes fluttered closed on her rosy cheeks, and she slid into an exhausted slumber.

Marianne stayed with her for a few more minutes, ensuring her sleep was restful before placing her tenderly in the cot. "Oh, Miss Ashbrook, that was wonderful," Doris said beaming.

Marianne smiled, bid her goodnight, and made her way from the room. The viscount was leaning on the wall by her door. The lit wall scone opposite him threw his features into a savage, stark relief. Something hot clenched low in her belly and her heart started to race.

He lowered his head when he saw her.

"Is Lizzie well?" he asked gruffly.

"Yes," she replied with a tremulous smile. "I suspect something bit her, the poor thing, and made her quite miserable. We placed a soothing salve on the spot, and she is now asleep."

"Good."

And the way he stared at her sent a flush through her entire body.

"I apologize for the manner in how I barged inside your room. I should have knocked more."

She fisted the front of her nightgown. "I was singing and thoroughly in my own head. Apology accepted, your lordship."

She reached her door and stole a glance at him. The

drafted man was still staring at her. "Was there a reason you waited, my lord?"

"To apologize."

"Which you already did, goodnight."

"And this…I also waited for *this*."

Before she could ask what he meant, his arms encircled her waist, and he spun her to face him. Warm strong hands cupped her cheeks, and he pressed his mouth to hers.

Oh! They faltered into remarkable stillness. He lifted his head and searched her face. "I want you…"

He placed a thumb against her lower lip, exerting the slightest pressure until her lips parted. "Your lordship!"

"Michael," he demanded, his eyes dark with arousal and something wicked. It wasn't the charmer or the gentleman who stood before her, but the unprincipled rake who would not care about marriage before taking her to his bed.

"I want you to call me by name."

Her breathing fractured, and her mind muddled. "Michael."

His name whispered through her heart in an intimate caress. He dragged her up against his body, almost violently and caught her mouth with his. There was no decency or hesitancy in the way he kissed her. It was deep, open mouthed, and shockingly carnal.

"Part those lush lips for me," he murmured hotly against her mouth.

She gasped, and his tongue swept inside. A small noise of pleasure broke from her throat. Marianne clasped his powerful shoulders as he lifted her in his arms and bypassed her door to his. Without releasing her, he managed to open his bedroom door and walked with her into his darkened chamber.

All the pent-up needs descended over her in an

exquisite burst of rebellious and chaotic desires. Their passionate kiss broke, she breathed raggedly, pressing trembling fingers against his mouth.

She stared into his eyes, and there she saw no apology for his wickedness…and the fact he was unleashing all of his debauchery with no care for her sensibilities or innocence. Her senses felt overwhelmed with fear…and such lust between her legs ached endlessly. As if he couldn't stop kissing her, he took her mouth again, their tongues tangling wildly. Unexpected hunger crawled over her skin with wicked heat. Her heart pounded an exhilarating yet terrifying tempo. Michael tumbled her atop the soft but very firm mattress, bracing his weight on his elbows. And he never released her lips from his drugging kisses. The warning alarms in her heart were drowned under a hot slide of arousal.

He dragged the hem of her nightgown over her legs and thighs, and a jerk of shock went through her. Oh God, she was naked beneath it! His knee slid between her legs, pressing against the sensitive mound at the secret heart of her.

She felt dazed with arousal, as a fever of need ignited in her body. One of his hands smoothed down her belly, brushed lightly over the curve of her hips, then delved between her thighs, finding a spot so sensitive that she gasped. Another violent shock went through her, hot and delicious. He caught her lower lip between his teeth and stroked over it with his tongue, lavishing her with soft nibbles and hot, urgent kisses.

His wicked fingers parted her and touched the intimate heart of her. She screamed into his mouth as a long finger slid deep.

"Ah hell," he said, his voice gravelly with arousal. "I knew you would be this wet…and *tight*."

His kiss offered no mercy, but she didn't want that tender consideration, responding to the violence of his kiss with artless wonder. She wrenched her mouth from him, buried her face in his throat, blushing furiously at his intimate touch.

"Don't hide from me. I want to see these beautiful eyes when you come undone for me."

He moved that finger and something twisted tightly, low in her belly. She arched her neck to allow him access, and he kissed along her throat. Marianne slid her fingers through his hair and gripped him tightly to her. As he stroked deep inside, aching hidden parts of her opened and wept unashamedly for him. "Michael," she moaned when he slipped another finger inside of her aching sex.

The stretch was painful, but then his thumb stroked over that tender bud. The sensations burst over her, pleasure so intense that she cried out. He disappeared from her, only to push her nightgown even higher. Before she could reach for him, he dipped and his mouth traced down her quivering belly, tongue flicking with depraved intention.

"Michael?" How breathless and wanton she sounded.

He split her legs wide to suck along her wet sex. It was wicked and lascivious, and she wanted more. His teeth scraped against that secret spot. Marianne convulsed, her back bowing from the bed. His fiendishly clever tongue pleasured her until she was hoarse from crying his name. The sweet, brutal ecstasy ravaged her until she came apart in a burst of such intense pleasure, her throat ached with a desperate need to scream.

He rolled with her, so she splayed atop him, and in a fever of need, she kissed along his bare throat. His groan reverberated through her. With impatient fingers she loosened his neckcloth, littering his chin, jaw, and mouth with hot kisses.

His laugh was strained, and he gripped her hips in an almost painful clasp.

"If you do not stop wriggling, I am going to embarrass myself like an untried lad."

Thank heavens, the necktie loose, his shirt and waistcoat opened partially. She pressed her lips against his chest, and a deep groan came from him. Marianne could not understand the needs pushing her to act in such a manner, only that she was desperate to assuage them. The place on his chest where her lips kissed glistened, and she leaned in again and bit down lightly.

"I am a man of carnal appetites," he said, his voice harsh with sensual intent. "I want to be gentle with you, but before the night is over, I want your lips around my cock. And you sitting atop me, riding my tongue."

The words and the guttural way he said them felt so filthy…so sinful…and a dark slide of lust blossomed through Marianne. She wanted to explore everything with him, give him her body unreservedly. *And what shall he give you but ruination?*

That unexpected thought had her wrenching free of his embrace and scrambling from atop him and off the bed. "Dear God, what madness has taken hold of me?" she cried in a low, shaking voice.

The viscount lifted a hand to her,

"Come here, Marianne."

She turned and ran from the room, her heart breaking into pieces. It had seemed so fine to think about her first kiss with the libertine! That had seemed so harmless…but what had happened just now, the desperate hunger she had felt to lay herself bare to him in all possible wanton ways.

The first time the devil had knocked she had succumbed frightfully easily.

Rushing to her room, she flung herself on the bed, pressing her face into the plush pillow.

"Oh, what have I done!"

CHAPTER 13

The connecting door to his chamber slammed with a resounding thud. With a groan, Michael slapped his open palm against his forehead. What the hell had just happened? He bloody well knew…he had decided to toss caution in the wind and seduce the ravishing Miss Ashbrook and damn everything else. For the first time in a long time, he felt like his old self. Wicked, carnal, and willing to indulge in all manner of debauchery.

Except he never believed it would have been an innocent who finally cracked that part of his soul that had been dying under *ennui*. How sweet and innocent she had tasted. The memory of her wild ripples fluttered over his skin, causing his heart to jerk. He blew out a harsh breath, his cock throbbing so hard he felt the pain of unfulfilled desires in his gut.

Before he could gather his scattered thoughts, the door was flung open, and Marianne rushed inside, her eyelashes damp with tears, her cheeks flushed a delightful pink. His cock jerked, and he silently hoped she had returned to finish what they had started.

"I am not immune to your kisses, Sir!"

"You're not?" he asked carefully, coming off the bed and stepping a bit to her. She seemed so rattled as if any moment she would flee and never return. The very thought was unbearable.

Her brows drew together in an agonized expression. "No! I find you frightfully attractive, and I *do* think about your kisses, but I must not lose my sense of self around you," she said, her voice cracking. "You must never kiss me in such a wicked manner again, or I fear I will not be able to stay under this roof a moment longer, your lordship. If I fall to ruin too, there are no consequences for *you*…while… while…" her throat worked on a swallow, and she fisted the front of her nightgown before her, wide eyes pleading at him.

In the depths of her green eyes, he saw the wanton in her, and with a few kisses, he knew he could have her beneath him, spread, and speared on his cock while he took them for a sinfully hot and wicked ride. The knowledge slammed into him, and he stumbled back as if he had been pushed. Never before had he seen such raw need and arousal and it was for him. Miss Ashbrook felt a similar desire for him. But in her eyes, he spied such fright his throat went dry.

"Please your lordship, keep your kisses to yourself. You are not likely to marry me after your ravishment so please save your attentions for someone who will be grateful for them."

"Why am I not likely to marry you?" As soon as the gruff words escaped his mouth, he felt regret. *Bloody hell!*

Her eyes were a wide pool of hurt in her flushed face. "You mock me, your lordship. A man of your wealth and connections wouldn't marry a lady of little consequence like myself. And I heard you in the gardens with Miss Benedict. You have no wish to marry. Do you refute it?"

"No," he said stiffly.

A flush suffused her pale and lovely face as is she were fevered. An inexplicable look of withdrawal came into her eyes. Michael ripped into the sensations darting through him and ruthlessly cut them off. "Forgive me, Miss Ashbrook, I assure you it will not happen again."

Her eyes searched his face for long moments, and whatever she saw eased the tension from her shoulders and the wounded look in her eyes.

"Thank you, your lordship."

"Michael, please," he replied. "I believe after tonight such formality is not called for. At least when we are alone."

She dampened her bottom lip with her tongue, and he looked away. When he returned his stare to her, she was over the threshold into her room. She glanced over her shoulders and said.

"Goodnight, your lordship." Then gently closed the door.

With a snarl, he started to dress without calling his valet Gibbs. Tonight, he did not need to be polished into the first stare of fashion. He was headed for the fighting pits. Michael was desperate to work out the unbridled frustration burning through his body. He could not find his outlet in another woman, simply because it felt wrong… unthinkable to tup another lady when his entire body and mind was consumed with Marianne Ashbrook.

Fully dressed once more, he exited his chamber and made his way down the winding staircase. The stable lads should already be sleeping, and he would not go to the mews and ready a horse. He would walk to his club. Perhaps the chilly night air would help him regain his bearings. Michael hardly knew what to do about the temptation of Miss Ashbrook. Now the entirety of his scheme to have her become Lizzie's governess felt stupid and fraught with peril.

IT HAD BEEN a week since the wicked viscount's kisses almost convinced Marianne to throw all sense of herself and propriety to the wind for pleasure. Days later she still retained the sensation of him making love with her, and he haunted her sensual dreams every night. The only relief was that his lordship appeared to be giving her a wide berth. And she knew he was avoiding her lest he succumb to the temptation of seducing her. Deep inside she realized that he was trying to behave like a gentleman, but that her very presence was making that hard for him. Perplexed by her own heightened emotions, she resented his absence, missing laughing and talking with him and just being able to see him.

But could she be so close to him and resist his skilled seduction? She felt quite unequal to the task. Shame rushed through her, and she hated that she had so little willpower against his ruthless kisses.

Last night she had been unable to sleep, and a wave of loneliness had engulfed her. For the longest time, she had lain on her side, staring at his connecting door, fighting the need to go to him. The taste of him had felt like an adventure Marianne was sure she would never experience with any other man.

"*Was this how you had felt, Lucy?*" she had whispered to herself in her darkened chamber. And that had been the restraint she had needed to turn her back to his door.

Still, sleep had eluded her, so she had put on her robe

and walked to the library, playing solitary chess on the plush oriental carpet by the fire. She closed her eyes as the memories washed over her.

"*Might I join you, Marianne*," the low drawl had come from a dark corner in the library.

She had not seen him and now her entire body had come alive. An unexpected shiver of anticipation had cascaded down her spine, but she had composed herself admirably. "*Yes*," she had murmured.

And he had sauntered over, with a drink in his hand, bruises on his knuckles and chin; he lowered himself to the ground, not commenting on the fact she was sprawled indecorously on her stomach. A deep silence, fraught with intimate peril had lingered, and they had played for over an hour with that quietness surrounding them.

"*You've been fighting*," she had said after a very long time.

"*I needed the distraction*."

They had stared at each other then, and she had numbly thought reading and spending more time with Lizzie was hardly a diversion for her.

"*Perhaps I need to take up bare-knuckle boxing too*," she had muttered, feeling aggrieved.

A dark smile, almost cruel in its sensual slant had shaped his mouth. He had taken a sip of his drink, his expression held a hint of mockery.

"*Checkmate*," she had murmured a few minutes later.

He had lifted his glass in a toast and downed the drink in one swallow. His expression had shifted and the libertine had peeked at her, his insolent gaze sweeping over her body, his mien taunting and derisive.

She had eyed him in uncertainty, feeling that in some strange way he was eluding her. Something about the viscount—the charmer, the kind and thoughtful gentleman, the dastardly reprobate—evoked confusing emotions within her. She fancied it had been his gray eyes which had stared at her so enigmatically that caused the ache inside her, the desire to partake of the wickedness lurking deep within them. Marianne had jumped to her feet. "*Goodnight, your lordship*," she'd said, and tried to walk away with some measure of serenity.

At the threshold, he had replied, "*Goodnight, Miss Ashbrook. I hope your sleep is pleasant and restful.*"

He had not meant it, and she had flushed and hurried away.

And now, she glanced down at the sheets of music he had left for her on the lid of the pianoforte. The thoughtful charmer was back. Perhaps after reading *The Knight of St. John*, she might play for an hour or so.

"Please, Sir, I am begging you. Is the viscount in?" a shrill voice cried.

With a frown, she carefully lowered the sheets of music and exited the music room.

"Please, Sir, do not close the door!"

The desperation in the unknown girl's voice arrested Marianne's movement.

"My lord is not in," the butler replied frostily, and once again attempted to close the door in the woman's face.

Gripping her book tightly, Marianne headed down the hallway, more curious than anything else. It was after eight in the evening. Who would come to call at such a scandalous hour and without an invitation?

The woman had thrust her hand forward, preventing the door from being closed.

The butler spluttered, outrage darkening his craggy countenance.

Marianne cleared her throat to garner their attention. "Is all well?"

He glared at her before his features smoothed. Impressive.

"A friend of yours perhaps, Miss Ashbrook?"

"No," she said with faint shock as she took in the woman's appearance.

Or more like a young girl, dressed in a garish pink dress with red ruffles and lace, with a plunging neckline. She had been caught in the rain, and rivulets of water ran from her hair to her neck, and there was an odd purple bruise around her throat and another on her cheek.

"Is that blood on your lips?" Marianne demanded, clutching the book even tighter to her chest.

The girl's lips trembled, and she sent a desperate glance behind her. Marianne moved closer and peered out in the sleeting rain. There was no-one else outside, but the girl's fear implied something else.

"Please, close the door," she said staunchly glancing at the butler.

He closed it with some firmness, clearly irritated by her command.

"Please, I must see Lord Worsley," the girl said a bit fretfully, twisting her hands together.

"Please, come with me," Marianne said. "There is a fire to warm yourself in the drawing-room." She glanced at the butler. "If you'll please ask Mrs. Barrett to arrange for some towels and tea, I am sure it will help miss…"

"I'm Evelyn," the girl hurriedly supplied with a smile that wobbled.

Soon they were in the drawing-room, the girl standing by the fire to dry her clothes and warm herself. She appeared increasingly frightened and kept glancing at the door.

"Lord Worsley is not here," Marianne said.

Evelyn closed her eyes in apparent defeat. "I…I am in

trouble, and he…he said I could come to him if I was ever in trouble."

"I see." It was not hard to decipher that she was a lady of disreputable reputation. "How did you meet Mic…Lord Worsley?"

The girl shrugged. "I tried to service him last week."

Marianne frowned. "I do not gather your meaning."

The girl stared at her with eyes that belonged to a woman twice her age. "You know how," she whispered, as if ashamed.

Marianne certainly did not know *how*, but she suspected it was in ways that might lead to a child. Feeling uncomfortable she said, "Perhaps you might return tomorrow. I will tell him that you came by before he leaves for the day."

The girl nodded, but she made no attempt to move. An expression of agonized doubt mixed with terror filled her face.

"What is it?" Marianne asked.

"I…If I go outside, I won't live to see the morning."

Marianne flinched, shock icing through her veins, her gaze once more settling on the bruises around the girl's throat and on her face. "That man who did this to you is outside?"

"No. I ran from him."

"Then—"

"But I have nowhere else to go. I lived at a boarding house run by him in Soho Square. I cannot go back, and… and Lord Worsley offered me employment at his club." She waved his calling card. "He gave me this so…I came here."

Marianne took the calling card from the girl. It bore the address of the club. "Why did you come here?"

"I…I followed him that day and saw that his carriage

took him here. I…when I ran just now this is where my head took me. Stupid," she muttered harshly. "I should have gone to the club."

"How old are you."

"Sixteen."

Marianne stared at the girl. Her youngest sister was sixteen and to think of her alone and in such a position was heartbreaking. But now she ran from one danger to another. The viscount's club was a place of wickedness. "Is there no other employment you could secure…instead of going to…to that place?"

The girl's eyes flashed. "Not many nobs would give a damn about girls like me. He promised respectable employment serving drinks only. I wouldn't…would not have to lift my skirts for anyone."

"I see." Marianne handed her the card. "I will call for the carriage to take you to the club."

She knew that earlier the viscount had walked when he left the house, so the equipage should still be in the mews. Relief lit in the girl's eyes, only to be quickly replaced with fear.

"Would you…would you accompany me, Miss?"

"Most assuredly not."

The girl nodded her understanding, but her expression remained bleak. She was keenly aware of the girl's fear and vulnerability. "Why do you wish my company?"

"Maybe he followed me. I could not tell for sure in the rain."

"Then I would argue the safest place would be for you to stay here until the viscount arrives home."

"Will that be soon," she asked eagerly.

Marianne took a deep breath. That she could not promise. Sometimes he did not return until noon the following day. "I am uncertain, perhaps a room—"

A throat cleared and she glanced up to see the butler standing in the doorway.

"This person cannot spend the night, Miss Ashbrook, not with Lizzie under the roof. It is unseemly. I am certain his lordship would never approve of such a thing!" he was affronted and scandalized.

Yet Marianne could not turn the poor girl away.

"If you will summon the carriage, Carlton," she said crisply. "I will accompany Miss Evelyn to the viscount's whereabouts. If you will have two or three footmen with us as well."

The butler looked at her as if she had lost a few of her senses, but he made no protest.

"Oh, thank you!" the girl said, clasping her hand before her.

"I'll not come inside with you. I shall merely show you to the front door."

The girl nodded.

Marianne smoothed the non-existent wrinkles from her dark blue gown with its high white lace collar. Certainly not a gown suitable to attend a club, but she had no intention of going inside so it would have to do. She hurried to her room and selected a hat with a black lace veil trimming that could be turned down to hide the top half of her face. She put on her dark pelisse and buttoned it tightly, she shivered at the thought of going out in the dark stormy night with possibly a violent man lurking out there.

She then went into the viscount's library and collected a silver-handled saber, and a large umbrella. If someone dared try to take this young girl on the trip from here to Mayfair, they would have to face her wrath and determination.

Making her way back to the drawing-room, she spied

Evelyn scarfing down tea and sandwiches. She blinked at the saber and a small smile curved her lips.

"We must depart now."

"Yes, Miss!" the girl jumped to her feet and followed Marianne who felt as if she were going into Hades and not just to the Devil's front door.

CHAPTER 14

Michael's evenings since that night, had consisted of dinner in the private hall, at his club, accompanied by a cigar, and a few drinks. He'd had these alone, ignoring the presence of his brother, his friends, and a few ladies who had sent him inviting smiles to join their tables. Nothing had moved him, except thoughts of Miss Ashbrook, which he refused to permit himself to indulge. The very memory of their encounter forced a groan to whisper from his lips. He *had* control…and he would damn well start to exercise it over his passions. After supping, he had spent a few hours going through the ledgers with Thomas, ignoring all his attempts at conversation, preferring the chill of silence. After that, he had retired to his private chambers on the third floor. However, the tranquility of his apartments had become tedious and irked him. He stood by the windows overlooking the streets, watching the carriages stop and pass by. Michael frowned, immediately identifying his own carriage as it pulled up outside his club. A footman jumped down and lowered the steps. A young girl, who glanced around her surroundings with a desperate air about her climbed out of the carriage.

He recognized her—It was the young girl who had tried to proposition him a couple weeks' ago in St. James's Square. He had given her a few banknotes and his business card, hating those who ruthlessly took advantage of poor girls in such a manner, trapping her into a harsh and painful life. She had taken the money, his card, and had melted away into the velvety dark. At times, he had felt as if she was following him, perhaps to try and lighten his pockets, but whenever he'd turned around, she had been hidden.

What in God's name was she doing in his carriage?

Another figure alighted, and he stepped closer to the window, every part of his body suddenly coming alive. *Marianne*. It was unpardonable, the heart-pounding reaction she roused in him. In her hands she gripped a saber and glanced around the poorly lit streets. Even from where he stood, Michael identified the determined set to her chin and the militant manner in which she gazed about. Whatever the hell was going on, she had ventured out prepared to do battle.

"Good God," he muttered, scanning the roads from his bird's eye view. He detected no immediate danger. An odd urgency coiled in his gut. He gripped the glass of brandy he'd been nursing, lifted it to his lips, and with one long swallow finished his drink, his gaze never leaving her.

Setting the glass down on the rosewood table, he exited his private apartments and bounded down the stairs to the lower floors. Michael ignored the undulating ripple through the crowd and those who called his name trying to capture his attention. His purpose was single-minded. Find out what had happened to cause Marianne to come to his club at this late hour. He glanced about and caught the eyes of Dorian Martin and two of his employees. Immediately they understood they should follow him, and to anticipate the unexpected.

Without waiting to see how quickly they were complying with his silent orders, Michael loped ahead and burst through the front doors of his club out into the streets without even bothering to don his coat. Miss Ashbrook gasped when she saw him, her lips parting, relief softening her mouth visibly under some sort of veil she was wearing. Pleasure warmed him from the inside out, but he composed his reaction and looked about. Still, the awareness lingered inside warming him with the knowledge that she had felt safe upon his arrival.

The young girl was staring at him, as if unsure how to proceed. Miss Ashbrook marched forward.

"Christ, is that a saber?" Dorian demanded from somewhere behind him.

Michael contained the rush of prideful amusement. "Miss Ashbrook is not the undecided, hysterical sort."

A low, suggestive whistle echoed from the man. "She is…stunning."

Her face was partially hidden, and from the roughness of Dorian's tone, Michael assumed it was her wonderfully lush and curved figure the man admired.

"So what sort is she?" he asked.

"The sort that is under my protection," Michael replied, just as she arrived in front of him.

Except from me…nothing can protect her from me.

She peered up at him. "Miss Evelyn showed up at h… your house, dreadfully afraid. It seems someone is out to hurt her."

The girl who hovered behind of her nodded, her eyes wide and fearful. She held out his card to him. "I am glad you came," he said softly. "Let's get off these streets and inside, you can tell me what has happened, but whatever it is, you can be assured of my protection."

"What…what if he comes to take me away?" the girl said fretfully.

Before Michael could reassure her of his power in these parts, Dorian stepped from behind him.

"He'll have to get through me first, Miss, and that is not likely to ever happen," he said with satisfied menace.

Few would ever consider tackling that giant wall of a man. Dorian had a soft spot for wounded birds, despising men who hurt the fairer sex in any manner. And from the way he was scanning the bruises on the girl's face and throat, the pain and fear in her eyes, even if that man did not come looking for her, Dorian would go hunting for him.

"If you'll come with me," he said gently. "You can go inside and eat something warm and quite delicious. The chef here is a Frenchie and believes he is a god. Then we can see about finding you a proper dress."

She clutched her throat and stared at him for several minutes, searching his face, and whatever she saw there, calmed her. For she took a deep breath and the fear all but leaked from her entire body. Dorian shrugged from his evening jacket and handed it to her. She slipped it on, though it swamped her tiny form and walked away with him after sending Michael a quick searching glance.

He nodded to show her that it was perfectly safe to go with Dorian, even though he suspected she knew that already. The other two men who had followed him outside walked off down the street, no doubt to assess if any of the carriages waiting in the queue had an enemy lurking within.

"She seemed so very afraid," Marianne said, biting her lower lip.

That nervous gesture set him on edge.

"Come inside," he said gruffly. "Until my men have ensured there is no danger about or anyone following you or the girl."

Through the thin material, he could see how wide her eyes had widened.

"Inside?" she squeaked. "In *there*?"

Exasperated humor rushed through him. "You sound like a little mouse."

She gasped in affront. "I do not! Nor will I go into that…that…place!"

"Fine. At least come into the hallway and allow me to gather my coat, hat, and walking stick. I will escort you home."

She glared at the hand he held out to her, and then at the large door behind him. Her fingers tightened on the saber. "There is no need for *that*, I—"

"There is every need," he said a bit forcefully. "I must see to your safety." *Always*. Then that devil in him whispered again…*except from me*.

She tapped a boot on the cobblestones. "Perhaps I might wait in the carriage."

"No, you may not."

She glanced about, and there came that biting of her lower lip again. "My reputation—"

His lips twitched. "Is safe. You are properly disguised, I assure you, Miss Ashbrook."

"Very well," she said primly. "Only as far as the hallway."

An odd sort of triumph slithered through him. She skirted around him and walked toward the door.

With a smile he followed her, leaned around and opened the door, allowing her to precede him inside. He let the heavy oak door to slam shut behind him. A din of laughter, screams of excitement, and music enfolded them. The majordomo reached for the umbrella, and she handed it to the man, but when he reached for the saber, she held it close to her chest.

"I believe I shall keep this with me."

"There is no danger in here," Michael promised her.

She gave him a pointed glare as if to say *he* was the danger.

Unable to halt the desire, he allowed the tips of his fingers to trail along the line of her jaw to the buttoned-up collar at her throat. Her pulse beat wildly against his thumb like the frantic wings of a captive bird. Would there ever be a time he looked at her without needing to touch?

"I believe I shall keep my saber," she said, her voice low but still possessing a breathless quality.

"Very well…" Then his lips curved. "I shall be back at once."

But he knew that irrepressible inquisitiveness would lure her further into his domain. The blast of pleasure that rocked through him from that wicked idea should have given him pause, but Michael silently hummed with satisfaction, unable to wipe the smile from his lips.

Your move…Miss Ashbrook.

MARIANNE WAS on the verge of doing something remarkably wicked. The sound of ribald laughter and the joyful refrain of a popular waltz tugged at her. She had always been drawn to beautiful music, like the piper with the pipe, luring her curiosity to fully appreciate the sweet sounds. What was hidden behind that dark red drape? What if she could take just a little peek, and truly see what the inside of a gambling den looked like? She snorted, quite irritated at her inquisitiveness. Yet, with a sense of alarm she realized she had moved closer, without consciously doing so. Marianne glanced over her shoulder to see the majordomo assessing her with something akin to amusement. She scowled at the man and looked back at the curtains the viscount had parted and disappeared through.

"Perhaps just a quick peek," she murmured. "Yes, I believe I shall! This is just another bit of adventure I will one day write in my memoirs."

Yes, because surely after living under the roof of Viscount Wicked, there would be something to record. She rolled her eyes at her own silliness, lifted her chin, squared her shoulders, gripped the saber, and walked forward. The thrill of something so positively improper tingled along her spine.

Taking a deep breath, she slipped her finger through the drapes, parted them, and stepped inside. The décor consisted of dark, rich paneled woods, green and silver velvet drapes lined the walls, and the luxurious oriental carpet that covered the floors and the staircase was a rich, vibrant red. Raucous joviality and conversation swirled around her, smoke wafted on the air, and there was an orchestra set now playing lively reels to the dancing couples. Toward the right of the large ballroom, fashionable men and women surrounded several tables, gambling, smoking cigars, and drinking. The games they played were unknown to her but seemed highly exotic as men dressed sharply in black trousers and jackets, white shirts and cravats shuffled cards with expert grace and rolled dice to the excitement of the gathered ladies in their lavish glittering evening dresses. Everyone and everything looked so fine and glamorous.

Dozens of glittering chandeliers hung suspended from the ceiling, their lights dancing off the hundreds of men and women in their finery. The ladies wore sparkling and exotic masks, while the men were unadorned. Couples embraced publicly on chaises longues, and those who danced were certainly closer than what was appropriate. Marianne's senses felt delightfully assaulted and she admitted she was painfully out of place.

"Ah, Miss Ashbrook…how I wish you had resisted," a dark murmur came from behind her.

She whirled around and peered into the provoking amusement shining in the viscount's eyes. Annoyed that he thought her a frightened ninny, she said, "I see nothing overly alarming."

His brow arched. "Ah…so these shocking display of intimacy and vulgarity do not appall you in the slightest? How interesting."

She could feel herself getting red.

"How prettily you blush."

That only made her face hotter. "How is Evelyn doing?"

"It will take a few minutes for me to check on her," he said with some gravity. "She was really scared and nastily banged up."

"Then go and reassure her that you'll help her, so that man, whoever he is, will never find her *and* that you'll also find her respectable employment."

He stared at her for a long moment. "I will." Then he melted away.

Her curiosity driving her, she sauntered forward,

looking at the different tables, staring for a few minutes here and there. A scream had her looking at another table where a young lady held a gloved hand over her mouth.

"Oh, Dear Lord, I won?" she glanced around dazedly.

"Yes," a portly fellow said. "Two thousand pounds!"

"My family might be saved?" she gasped and then burst into tears.

Everyone stared at her for a few seconds, then went back to their game, dismissing the woman. The young lady was, however, shaking like a leaf.

Marianne went over to her. "Are you well?"

"I think I've won a fortune, but he won't allow me to keep it, will he?" she said in a pained whisper.

"Who shall not allow it?"

"My uncle!"

She gasped as if she had said too much. "Please forget I said it."

Marianne gripped her gloved hand. "You were very brave to have come here and try…try your chance at lady luck."

The girl nodded as if she desperately needed the assurance that she had done the right thing.

"I risked my reputation and my safety…I risked *everything* to save my family."

She placed a hand around the girl's shoulders and led her to a quieter section of the gambling den. It took bypassing several tables and going behind a green velvet curtain, but thankfully a few chaise longues, tables, and chairs were there and unoccupied.

They sat on the chaise closest to the fire. Feeling overly warm, Marianne removed her coat and placed it on a chair. Then she turned to the girl, very perturbed to see she was still crying and twisting her fingers together.

"I gather you fear your uncle will chastise you for coming here?"

The girl's face crumpled, and more tears came. "More likely, he will steal this money as he stole my small inheritance from me! My sisters and I live off his goodwill and we are all of age but with little choice. I have risked coming here…hoping for a chance, but I never dreamed…*oh* I never truly imagined I might win!"

Marianne patted her arm and offered the girl a gentle smile. "There is no need for you to worry. Lord Worsley will see that you receive your winnings and even protect them for you. Why I even believe should you ask him to invest a portion of it for you so you could secure your sisters' future."

"He would?" the girl asked with considerable surprise. "The Viscount Wicked would do that…for me?"

Marianne nodded firmly. "He is most kind and thoughtful."

A choked sound came from behind her, and she turned to see the man who had gone away with Miss Evelyn.

"Good evening, ladies, I am Mr. Dorian Martin. Might I escort you to the private dining hall on the second floor?"

They stood, the curtains parted once more, and Michael appeared. Her heart leaped, and a quiver of something hot went through her belly.

The girl dipped into a curtsy, "My lord!"

Mr. Martin cast the viscount a sidelong stare. "Miss… this young miss here was advising our most recent winner that you would do whatever it takes to ensure her uncle does not try to take her winnings away because you are the kindest and most thoughtful of men," Mr. Martin said with such incredulity, Marianne scowled at him.

"His lordship *is* most kind and—"

"Thank you, Miss Ashbrook," the viscount murmured

softly, his face carefully composed. "Dorian if you will take this young miss to Thomas. He'll draft her banknotes, and please let her appraise you of the situation." Then he stared at the girl who was no longer crying but staring at him with grateful awe. "And of course, if Miss Ashbrook has promised, I will see that this uncle does not see a shilling of your money."

The girl clasped her hand around her middle. "And that I might get away with my sisters safely? Somewhere he might not find out?"

Michael sent her an unfathomable look, but then said to the girl, "Yes."

"Truly?" the girl gasped.

"Truly," he replied softly.

Mr. Martin blinked several times, then looked at Marianne as if she had snakes writhing from her hat.

And at that moment, Marianne felt her heart tumble over in a way it never had before. The feelings shivering through her… they rose in a sweet, gentle swell, sensations she hardly knew what to do with until they encompassed her entire being.

I love you…she cried silently.

She was hardly aware when the girl profusely thanked her and melted away with Mr. Martin, leaving her alone with Michael.

"If you would grab your coat. I will escort you home."

Yet his eyes spoke a challenge for her to stay here… even if but for a moment, to bask in another kind of adventure.

"No," she said, "Perhaps I might stay…perhaps this ordinary country girl might see and experience something wonderful tonight."

Her madness was complete.

Instead of the triumph she expected to see, his gaze

softened, and something impossibly possessive yet tender glowed in the dark silver of his eyes. He cupped her cheek and lifted her face to his. "My dear Miss Ashbrook... Marianne...there is *nothing* ordinary about you."

Then he claimed her mouth in a kiss of marauding passion.

CHAPTER 15

Marianne's heart pounded, and desire swirled through her veins. A soft nip at her lower lip, then she parted her lips in a soft moan of complete surrender, and his tongue slipped into the depths of her mouth. A sharp bite of pleasure gripped her as his tongue mated with hers. With a muffled moan, she clasped his shoulders, tipped on her toes to meld her lips to his more passionately.

He released her, quite reluctantly, and she stepped back. His sharp cheekbones were flushed, and the look in his eyes had her glancing away. Inside, she felt weak with need and reckless desires. Gripping the edges of her skirt, she said the first thing that popped into her mind, "I cannot imagine why Mr. Martin acted so astonished to learn of your kindness. I know it…and he has been in your employ long enough, I presume, so why shouldn't he know of it?"

It occurred to her moments later that she was babbling.

"Here…I am a different man."

"In what manner?" she dared to ask, though she could feel the difference in his intensity.

"At home…" His throat worked on a swallow.

Her breath caught. *Home*. Such yearning rose to choke her like thick smoke. How that word filled her with such acute longing. And for the first time, she admitted one of the things she hungered for was a love that defied the odds for herself. And that it was with this man she imagined and dreamed for so much. *Silly little heart.*

"At home, I am different. Here I am the purveyor of sin. I climb in the ring, and I bare-knuckle fight with the best and toughest of men. Here I am the Viscount Wicked, and I do not hide from the reputation which gave me that name but embrace it."

"And I am not afraid of it," she said with aching honesty. She had never imagined she could be so bold.

He caught her hand, and pressed a hot kiss to her palm. "Dance with me."

She feared they would never meet again, for she knew he would never marry her. She would dream forever of him, and Marianne knew she would live with regret her whole life if she never experienced all that she could with this man. "Yes," she breathed and followed as he drew her onto the ballroom floor.

He tugged her scandalously close, and she gave a quick glance to ascertain no-one else was observing the formal respectable conventions. For the space of a heartbeat she could not speak. A startling rush of need arrowed to her aching heart. Heat curled low in the pit of her stomach, jolting her. She was so tempted to tip up on her toes and lick his lips. Right here in front of everyone!

A blistering need to feel his arms around her surged through her. "Hold me closer," she murmured, thinking she might never have the chance to indulge so wickedly ever again.

His eyes became impenetrable, but his fingers clenched, and he tugged her in so much closer. Marianne felt the slight trembling in his frame, and a sense of awe gripped her. He struggled with wanting her, and sensing it, she did not withdraw or have mercy on him but lifted a hand to his face so she could swipe her thumb across his bottom lip.

His lips were so soft. How bold she was. He groaned, and the sound whispered through her.

"Mis…Mari…Ashbro…." he broke off, a deeper flush staining his cheekbones.

"I made you stammer," she said with gentle amusement. "Am I the first?"

"Everything I am feeling now…*you* are the very first to inspire them, and I suspect the only woman who will ever do so."

He seemed almost bewildered to have admitted that. But inside…inside Marianne's long-denied needs swirled to the surface with hot, and debilitating hunger. She felt enslaved by the desire in his eyes, and the gentle tremble of his fingers. Her heart clamored harder, sending dizzying rushes of desire coursing through her veins.

"Do I take you to my rooms upstairs?" he asked gruffly. "Or do we dance?"

An odd emotion erupted through her heart. "We dance," she whispered as he twirled her into an elegant spin before catching her closely to his body once again. She twirled gracefully, the rousing strains of the violins igniting delight in her. It was even more glorious than when she had waltzed with him at the duchess's midnight ball. She felt free to clasp his shoulders, to peer into his eyes without wondering if those watching would think her too forward. Around her, other couples whirled laughing and twirling, soaking up the decadence of the ballroom.

Marianne danced at least four sets with the viscount until her feet ached, and sweat beaded her brows, and even her lips trembled from too much laughter. Then…and only then, she stared up into his eyes and said, "Now take me to your rooms, and perhaps I shall taste brandy."

He faltered in stillness, as if he were afraid she would take back the words. Then he gripped her hand and led her through the crowd, up three flights of the winding staircase without breathing a word. Her tongue would not loosen, and her heart hammered more with each step. For Marianne knew…once in that room he would kiss her and do delicious, wicked things to her.

And she wanted to experience every decadent thing he would do. Her common sense tried to reassert itself, but the very knowledge that she might never be with him again tore through it. All her reserve crumpled to her feet. He opened the door to his apartments, and she gained a quick impression of dark furniture, rich brocade drapes, and a roaring fire. He closed the door, cupped her cheek, and pressed his mouth to hers, so gently her heart fluttered.

A rough, low, and hungry sound spilled from him. "I cannot…I have not the willpower to stay away from you."

How tortured he sounded.

A sweet, sharp pain throbbed in her chest. "Then don't," she whispered breathlessly. "I cannot have you forever, so I will take this moment in time." Her stomach fluttered with nerves, but her heart ached with passionate desire.

He drew her into his arms, pressed a kiss to her forehead, and they stayed like that for a breathless moment. Then he cupped her chin and lifted her face to his. The raw force of his mouth possessed her, the strength of his hunger catching her unawares, yet she eagerly responded with burgeoning passion. She couldn't think, she didn't want to think, only to *feel.* Michael lifted her into his arms; she gripped his shoulders as he walked with her a few paces and then slowly lowered her. The back of her knees brushed against something, and a quick glance revealed it to be a bed.

She almost fainted when he started to shrug from his clothes, his gaze never leaving hers. His jacket, then his waistcoat, his cravat was tugged at with such impatience! Then his shirt.

Marianne sucked in an audible breath. "You are beautiful, Michael."

Sharp and svelte muscles delineated his chest down to his waist. Although she knew he would be considered a man of leisure, the body he was revealing was lithe and beautifully muscled, showing not an ounce of fat. He dropped to his knees before her, his dark blond head bent, as he lifted her feet, one after the other and removed her slippers. She shuddered, her body throbbing under the sensual onslaught his fingers evoked as they trailed up her legs to her shin, and higher to unpin her garters. Then he rolled down her stockings, slow and sensual, and tugged them from her feet. He stood and turned her around, where he undid the buttons of her dress. In silence, he removed all of her garments, never fumbling as if he had done this so very often before.

The reminder that she stood in a room with a rake of the first order reared its head, but she closed her eyes, admitting painfully that she was not here because of *his* seduction, but because of how much she wanted to feel this with him…if only once. The notion of being so wicked and improper had a strange heat beating in her blood. As her stays, chemise, drawers, and crinoline fell away, shyness gripped her.

"Let me see you," he breathed.

Marianne bit her lower lip and turned to him, painfully aware she was naked!

His chest rose on a deep inhalation, pleasure and admiration lighting his silver gaze. "I've never seen another equal to you…and I daresay I never will. You are beautiful, Marianne."

A sense of vulnerability and empowerment slid through her veins in equal measure. She lifted her hand and removed the pins holding her hair until her tresses tumbled over her shoulders, breasts, and back.

This time, when he drew her closer, Michael took her lips in a kiss of violent tenderness. They kissed endlessly, his fingers tangling in her hair as he held her close for his ravishing. He released her lips and kissed along the jaw down her neck and over her collar bone. He arched her, dipped his head, and licked her nipple. How naughty it felt…that slow, hot, glide of his tongue across that throbbing peak.

His fingertips brushed lightly and gently along her exposed sex. Then he was there, and Marianne's thoughts splintered under a painful rush of arousal as he rubbed at her nub of pleasure. Her body responded violently on a shudder of delight. His fingers never stopped moving, never stopped touching her. His fingers slipped over her aching nub with even more firmness, and then he pinched down. Her nub got harder, more sensitive, yet his questing fingers never stopped their slippery caresses as she trembled with powerful quakes and her breathing became fast and urgent.

Relentless waves of pleasure engulfed her entire body, and a wild cry spilled from her throat. She hadn't expected anything like this when they came together. The room spun, and she became distantly aware he had lifted her and placed her in the center of the bed.

Her hands reached for him, but he was not there, instead he was crawling down her body. Marianne's entire body blushed when he parted her legs. He cupped her buttocks in his palms, tilting her hips and pressing his mouth to her aching sex. She cried out, gripping the sheets beneath her, twisting them. His kisses were sinful… deep and erotic. She rocked against him, wrapped in steaming sensuality, breathless cries echoing from her lips. The stark sensation went on and on, consuming her with pleasure.

He moved away from the bed, and from the rustling sounds she gathered he removed his boots, trousers, and stockings. Then the bed dipped, Michael rose above her, his sensuality carved into his handsome face. Her breath caught at the stark male hunger in his gaze. She gripped his shoulders and instincts made her wrap her legs around his thighs and bury her face in the crook of his neck. She could feel the pounding rhythm of his pulse, and she nipped lightly at his throat. Suddenly he was there, where the ache was most terrible. His hips pushed, and her body was wet, soft, and yielding, accepting the hard length that surged deep inside, but even so, her muscles quivered to accommodate his thickness. "Michael," she gasped at the sharp pain.

He cupped her cheek, peppering soft kisses over her lips. "I am sorry," he soothed. "It will soon pass."

Her flesh burned as she adjusted to the thick invasion of his body into hers, and she didn't think she could believe him. But then, he reached between their bodies and rubbed that spot.

She shivered in his embrace, unintentionally arching and driving him even deeper. Marianne moaned, her nails biting into his sweat-slicked shoulders. Then he started to move.

Oh! It was glorious.

Marianne lost her breath; she lost all control of her body. Sensuality hazed through her mind, and she lifted her hips, eager for the pleasure whispering through every part of her. He drew out and then plunged deep. Again. And again. And again, until she lost even the ability to moan. It was the most nerve-wracking pleasure she had ever felt. Marianne could only hold him to her as he rode her through the storm. She sank her teeth into the muscle of his shoulder as exquisite sensations sliced through her body. Each deep thrust ignited a burst of fire deep down in her stomach until sweet, mind-shattering ecstasy blew through her, and she unraveled with a sharp cry.

With a deep groan, he pulled from her, before releasing his seed on her quivering stomach. Panting, he dropped his forehead to hers. Even in the dim light of the fire, she saw the shock written on his face. And she understood. Never had she dreamed this was possible with two people coming together in intimacy.

After several moments he climbed off the bed, the flickering fire cast dancing shadows over his naked form. He returned with a damp washcloth and cleaned her gently, before coming down on the bed and tugging her into his arms. She closed her eyes, and her breath released in a long sigh.

"In a few more minutes, I am going to take you home," he said softly. "Then I am going to take you into my room, place you on my bed, and love you all over again."

She felt the tenseness as he waited for her reply. She lifted her head from the crook of his arm and looked into his eyes. Then with a smile, she simply said,

"Yes."

CHAPTER 16

Marianne awoke slowly, her senses alive, her body pliant and sated. *I am ruined.* A mix of emotions assaulted her senses—fear, joy, and a sweet, tender feeling that felt frightfully like love. It wasn't the wicked lure of the club which had distorted her senses. The feelings were still there in her heart, solid and immovable. She shifted slightly on the bed, lifting the heavy arm banded around her waist, and turned to face Michael.

How peaceful he appeared in sleep. She traced his brow and jawline tenderly. Marianne had given herself passionately without shame or reservation to a man who was not likely to marry her. While she felt no regret, she knew they could not decide to live a life of sinful decadence without consequences.

His eyes flickered open, and her smiled wobbled.

"How pretty you are," he murmured.

His words brushed against her skin like a caress, and she craved more. With a soft cry, she pressed against him and kissed him most ardently.

"Why are you crying?" he demanded gruffly.

And it was then with some alarm she tasted the salt of her tears. "It is of no significance," she said against his lips.

He rolled with her, drawing her underneath him with practiced eased. "Everything about you is important to me, tell me."

She slipped her hands around his nape, but she could not bear to ask him 'what now?'. She had been the one to visit his den of ill repute, and she had willingly surrendered to his ravishment. A desperate feeling of unreality crept through her. They had made love, at least three incredible times.

"I do not like the fear in your eyes."

"I daresay say it is normal to feel anxious in this situation. I have never done this before, you know."

His lips curved ever so slightly, and he pressed a gentle kiss to her brow. "Do not worry, I will take care of you."

Her heart shattered into pieces Marianne doubted would ever be put back together. He would take care of her. She knew what *that* meant. *As his mistress*.

Pain lanced through her—sudden and breathtaking. Her lips trembled against his as he kissed her with deep intensity. Her heart was pounding so loudly that she could hear nothing else. He pulled down the collar of the nightgown she had donned sometime in the night and slipped his fingers below the hem of her gown. She inhaled roughly, her breasts rising and falling with her quick breathing.

The smell of him aroused a wonderful sensation within her, and between her legs, it ached. The realization that this moment must be the very last she spent with him broke something inside of her. Thrusting her fingers through his hair, she melded their mouths together fiercely.

His groan vibrated deep inside her, and a need radiating low in her belly engulfed her entire body. He reached between them and something thick and heavy nudged at her entrance. Penetration was immediate. Marianne cried out into his still ravaging mouth at the fullness of his invasion. That burning pressure soon faded to unbridled desire. He was rough in the way he took her, but she did not mind, and Marianne gloried in every pounding thrust until she fragmented under the onslaught of ecstasy.

Once again, he released his seed outside of her body, cleaned her, and held her onto his chest. They lay on their sides, facing each other, their breaths trembling against each other's lips, sweat slicking their bodies.

"I love you," she said achingly.

He stiffened for several moments before he lowered his forehead to her. The fire had burned low, casting the room in more shadows than light, hiding his expression from her. He shifted, rolled onto his back, and curved her into the side of his arms.

"What I feel for you I do not know how to define," he said softly. "I do know what I feel for you Marianne—this hunger to be beside you, kissing you, laughing, and just conversing, I have never felt with another."

She made no reply, battling back the emotions crashing through her. They were not words of love, and she was uncertain if it was that she wanted from him at this moment. Or was it a reassurance that she meant more to him than a mistress.

How desperately silly I am.

He held her until she fell into a deep slumber, a most disquieting pain in her heart.

The bright sunlight shining through the drapes in her chamber woke Marianne. She turned, feeling remarkably exhausted and tender all over. She sat up in the bed as the wicked memories of the night came rushing in. *Good heavens!* She clasped her heated cheeks and glanced wildly around them. A soft sigh escaped her as she noticed that she was in her own chamber. She had not felt when the viscount…Michael had carried her to her bed.

She hurried from the bed and rang the bell for Harriet to attend her. Almost two hours later, she felt refreshed after taking a bath and eating luncheon. It had been embarrassing to realize it had been after one in the afternoon. None of the staff had commented on her late rising, but Marianne had blushed infernally with every curious stare she met.

Worse, there was a heaviness in her heart that grew by the minute. Slipping into the nursery, she faltered on the threshold to see Michael sitting in a rocker with Lizzie in his arms. Marianne hadn't realized he was in residence. She had simply assumed he was out. Doris was absent, and Marianne was glad for it. A wave of shyness fell over her. He glanced up, and a flare of lust entered his gaze…and also tenderness.

"I exhausted you," he murmured, carnal knowledge of her gleamed in his eyes. She felt hot and achy and couldn't break the intimacy of his lingering gaze. "I will be more mindful next time not to take you four times in one night."

A violent wave of mortification seized her, and she gasped. She glanced over her shoulder to ensure no-one was about and could have possibly overheard his scandalous remarks. Then his words sunk in. *Next time.*

He stood and came over to her. Michael held Lizzie to his chest with one arm, and with his other hand, placed a finger under her chin and lifted her gaze to his. "Are you well?"

"Yes," she replied, fighting the urge to blush with a ruthless will.

His dark gaze searched hers as if he did not believe. "I promise we will talk tonight…about everything. I must leave soon. I have a few investors I have to meet with and I am expected by Wycliffe and Viscount Shaw at the club. Come to the club tonight. I've arranged for you to be taken to a modiste who will outfit you in the latest fashionable modes. I've ordered that for each gown, at least a dozen, a mask should be made to complement it."

Oh, God. It was worse than she imagined. "Michael…" and suddenly Marianne knew she had to leave because everything inside of her wanted to say yes and to live freely with him in wanton decadence. For him, she would lose all sense of herself because she loved him so very much.

"What is it?"

She took Lizzie from him. "Go to your meetings."

He pressed a quick, hard kiss to her lips, and then a tender one to Lizzie's forehead, before leaving and ringing for his valet. Lizzie came awake, and Marianne hugged the baby close to her, the pain in her heart making her tremble. She could no longer stay under his roof, or every night she would submit to his wicked ravishment until she ended up with child. Then she would be in the very same position her sister and countless women who had fallen for the charms of a rake found themselves in.

It pained her so to leave Lizzie, but Marianne was completely assured that Michael loved her as he would a daughter. She had been in the viscount's home for over six weeks and that bounder Thomas had never called again to see Lizzie, yet not a day had gone by, when the viscount had not visited her in the nursery.

Doris entered, and Marianne handed Lizzie over after pressing a kiss to her brow. It was not farewell forever, but when she had mastered this weakness she had for the viscount, she would visit, and only to see her niece.

Several minutes later, she sat in the carriage with her two valises and a hatbox, as it rumbled toward Grosvenor Square. The coach stopped at the stately townhouse of the duchess Wycliffe, and Marianne alighted with the aid of a footman. Lifting her chin, she made it up the stairs, and the butler allowed her entrance and led her to the drawing-room. A few minutes later the duchess entered, her eyes worried.

"Marianne!" she held out her hands, and Marianne clasped them.

"It is such a pleasure—" Sophia started to say.

Marianne was appalled when she burst into raw, ugly tears, all the agony she had been trying to suppress eating inside her heart.

"Oh, dear," Sophia said. "What has that wicked bounder done?"

Marianne desperately tried to gather her composure. "Nothing that I did not want or invite," she admitted with a blush. "Please do not blame his lordship…but I cannot be his mistress."

"Of course not! You are a respectable girl."

"I must leave…for Bath. Will you help me?" Marianne supposed she could take the train and then the stagecoach, but she needed to be away much quicker than that.

Shrewdness glinted in the duchess's eyes. "Most certainly. And I shall not tell a soul to where you are headed."

"Thank you, Sophia," Marianne said with a tremulous smile.

No need for this heartache, she fiercely reminded herself. It was a deliberate choice she had made. To take a wonderful night of passion for herself and then to leave. So, oh why did she feel as if she were slowly dying inside? The ache of loss felt terrible, and she was mortified that she was crying like an idiot, for she'd not had the viscount's affection or tender regard in the first place to lose it. But her heart and mind did not listen, and as the duchess made arrangements with her coachman, a maid to chaperone her, and a couple of footmen for protection, Marianne tried to pick up the tattered pieces of her heart knowing her time with Michael had altered her forever.

MICHAEL ENTERED his darkened townhouse a few minutes after midnight, his brother hot on his heels. The servants were abed, and Michael hurried down the hall, taking the stairs two at a time to reach the upstairs landing.

"I'll be in the drawing-room," a disgruntled Thomas called out.

Michael had sensed something had been wrong and had not wanted to wait until his return in the early morning hours. His brother, who had demanded that he most urgently needed to talk to him, had followed in his carriage. Michael made no reply and hurried down the hallway, the cold, empty feeling, which had gripped him in the club mounting, tightening across his chest. He opened the door to Marianne's chamber to find it dark with no fire lit. The empty feeling dug deeper into his heart, and the swell churned and tossed, wanting to drown him.

Closing the door, he headed to the nursery and entered. A cozy fire roared, and a lamp was also lit. Doris was curled in a chair, reading a book. She glanced up at him and lowered the novel.

"Where is she?"

Doris stood. "Your lordship…Miss Ashbrook left this

afternoon after saying her farewells. She…she said she will not be returning."

Her words were a brutal punch to his chest. He gripped the doorknob until his knuckles whitened. "I see. Thank you, Doris." Michael closed the door and leaned against it for several moments.

She had left without even a farewell. He recalled the pain in her gaze this morning…how haunting and sad he had thought she appeared. Several times he had thought to let her go, knowing she could not stay under his roof forever. He'd never known such sweet torture as her kisses, her sighs, the sound of her laughter, and the pleasure in her arms. He had never felt joy and satisfaction equal to being with her, and he doubted he ever would. Hours later he could still taste the heady scent of her passion, hear her pleasure-filled cries, feel the care in her touch as she had wrapped her arms around him and held him tightly to her. A rough breath escaped him, and he made his way to his room and stumbled onto the bed.

The crinkle of a paper sounded, and he felt around until his fingers grasped at something. He lurched to his feet, noting it was a letter. The fire in his room burned too low for him to discern the words. He bounded down the stairs and into the drawing-room where a roaring fire and two lamps were lit.

Dear Michael,

It breaks my heart to leave you and Lizzie. I had not been aware that I felt unmoored in this world, a ship without an anchor, or any sense of direction to where I must go. Being with you these past weeks have been a pleasure and have revealed much about my character and desires I did not know before. I found a friendship with you that was wonderful, and I also thank you for the time you allowed me with dear Lizzie. It made our parting less bittersweet, and I am no longer haunted by what the future will hold for her. I have the utmost faith you will care and love her and protect her at any cost.

It is one of the reasons I love you. I am not ashamed or afraid to admit that, but I also know you are not capable of returning my sentiments. I knew you were a rake of the first order when I gave myself to you, but it does not mean I will live as your mistress, for I know my worth. I do hope perhaps one day in the future we might be genuine friends.

Farewell,

In the event a dastardly villain should ever find this letter, I shall sign with,

Yours, Miss A!

Michael carefully folded the letter after reading it for the third time. Marianne had left, and he could already feel the loss of her smiles and tinkling laughs. He rubbed a hand over his chest, where his heart damn well ached.

"Is everything well?" his brother asked, taking a sip of his drink. "You rushed upstairs as if the devil chased you and now you are just staring broodily at that blasted note!" Thomas said, his tone very miffed. "Is it…is something wrong with the child?"

Now he sounded unsure and a bit apprehensive. Michael did not bother to reply, Marianne's words resounding in his mind.

I do not want to be your mistress…I know my worth.

An unknown feeling swelled inside of him. It took him a while to identify it as pain. Raw and scraping at his insides. She had run believing him to only care that she was in his life to slake his baser needs. *Bloody hell.* He did know her worth. She was an irreplaceable treasure.

"Good God, man, what is wrong? You appear as if someone has died," Thomas said, with a scowl.

Michael went over to the sideboard and poured himself a splash of brandy, truly shocked to see that his hand trembled. "Miss Ashbrook has left."

"Is…is that bad?" his brother asked.

Michael faced him. "Very much so. I…I cannot imagine life without her, it seems."

Thomas's eyes widened, and his brother's start of shock was almost comical. "What does that mean! She is not suitable to be your wife!"

Michael lifted the glass to his lips and downed it in one swallow. "Why not?"

"Well!" Thomas spluttered. "You are Viscount Worsley, your wealth is unmatched even by dukes! What does she have to offer?"

"Her kindness recommends her," Michael said gruffly. "Her utter joy for life and living, the way her eyes light up when she sees me, the beauty of her heart. The way she makes me feel…" *God.* He scrubbed a hand over his face. He sounded like a damn moon-calf poet.

"I see," Thomas said a bit weakly, a contemplative look in his eyes.

Last night she had whispered, "I love you," and every place inside him that had been cold, empty, and frustratingly blank had been filled with a sense of wonder. Pieces which had been cracked and damaged slowly came back together healed throughout the day. He hadn't been able to concentrate on his meetings to his friends' great amusement. His mind had been crowded with images of her…a bright smile, a cheeky wink, the lascivious way he had taken her, her soft lips…everything about her had been imprinted on his heart.

I know your worth.

Her letter did not mention if she would be open to an offer to be his wife, and doubt quivered through him. He realized then he did not know what she hoped for in the future and if she would have any space for him in it. Then he recalled her greatest dream was for a family of her own and to live life freely. *I can give you that, Marianne.* The surety of it bloomed through him.

But would she want him? A man she believed to be only a rake and wicked libertine?

"I must go to her," Michael muttered.

"The hell you say!"

He had forgotten Thomas was still in the drawing-room. He looked at his brother, noting the misery in his eyes and the frown on his mouth. And suddenly Michael understood. "You love Lucy Ashbrook."

His brother was silent for a long time. "Yes, I do."

"You are a damn coward for not doing anything about it."

Thomas's gaze snapped to him, and in his brother's eyes Michael spied a deep shame and pain. "I am…I fear there is nothing I can say to her that will allow her to forgive me. And…I am *engaged*."

Michael thought how different his brother was. Michael did not give a damn what society thought about his choices. He wanted Miss Marianne Ashbrook, and the only thing that could keep him from her would be the lady's objection.

"If you wish to break your engagement…do so!"

"And the scandal?" Thomas demanded, with a hopeful look in his eyes.

"Damn the scandal," Michael said ruthlessly. Then the

image of Marianne's face came to him, and in her eyes, he saw abject censure and disappointment. *Bloody hell!* Before knowing her, he wouldn't have even been bothered by the consequences of a broken engagement to the girl and her family. But Marianne expected him to be kind and thoughtful. Michael scowled down into his drink.

Ah, Marianne how you've altered my heart.

"If you need my permission or blessings to go for Lucy Ashbrook, you are a damn fool. But if you do need it, you have it. I will also speak with Lord Kenwood."

The glass dropped from Thomas's hands, and he raked his fingers through his hair, mussing the strands. "I might really go for her?"

"Yes."

His brother closed his eyes. "That is what I wanted to speak to you about," he admitted hoarsely. "I have known for the last few weeks I cannot marry Lady Sarah. Miss Ashbrook does not know it, but I wait by the park daily to catch a glimpse of her and…and Lizzie. And each day, I think that should be Lucy pushing our daughter in her perambulator. I then imagine how Lucy must be devastated to not have her child with her…and I feel wretched. I cannot marry Sarah, but I do not want to hurt another lady. But Lucy! She haunts me, Michael!"

And he understood, for everything in him felt owned by Marianne Ashbrook.

CHAPTER 17

Lucy had been set up in a five-bedroom townhouse in Bath near Camden Place. She had a butler, maids, a cook, a lady's maid, and even a footman! Her sister seemed quite accepted by the society there, considering she was called upon daily by many of the most respected notables residing in the town. Although now she was known as Lucy Elliot, the name chosen from one of her favorite novel heroines. Lucy had assumed widowhood and had made a friend with another charming girl who was the daughter of a baronet.

Lucy had also applied her heartbreak and experiences to write a gothic romance novel which she had just finished. Marianne had stayed up for a few nights reading, because she found it hard to sleep at all. The very idea was splendid, and in the story of the novel, the dastardly villain who had gotten the heroine pregnant after trapping her in a tower, came back and married her. It was easy to see the desperate dreams Lucy still held in her heart and Marianne had wept for them both and their foolish hearts.

Marianne had been with her sister for a week now, and

each day she felt as if loneliness would suffocate her. Her sister's company was wonderful, but the pain in her heart lingered too deeply. Marianne did not like it at all and hid from the overwhelming feelings by reading. A knock sounded on her bedroom door, and before she could answer, it was opened, and Lucy strolled in, looking the very picture of elegance. She wore a pale-yellow muslin dress with a cinched waist and close-fitting bodice trimmed with white lace, and a matching hat was perched atop her curls.

"I plan to call upon Venetia, and then we shall visit the pump room, would you like to accompany me?" Lucy said with a bright smile.

Marianne attempted to smile and failed miserably. "I do not feel equal to the task. Perhaps another time."

"You have been saying this to me for the last few days. I can tell that something is awfully wrong," Lucy cried, coming over to sit on the bed. "You have been very morose but endeavoring to be brave. I can see the pain in your eyes because it is what I have in my heart daily! Will you not confide in me? Is it Lizzie…" Lucy's voice broke, and she clasped her gloved hands in a tight grip.

With a gasp, Marianne sat up and grabbed her sister's hands between hers. "Of course not! Lizzie is…Lizzie is wonderful!" Then she took a deep breath. "There is something I must confess to you…and I did not want to because I cannot bear hurting you more."

Green eyes, very much like her own, lifted her to Marianne's and she saw how much Lucy had grown in the strength she spied there.

"Tell me," she said quietly.

And then she revealed it all.

Lucy swayed but then held onto her wits with admirable composure. "Thomas…he is not Lord Worsley and Lizzie is living with the viscount, but he is her uncle, and *that* is where you have been for the last several weeks?"

Marianne took a deep breath. "Yes."

"Oh, Marianne, I cannot credit he would deceive me so. I love…I loved him, not the idea of his title and wealth." She swiped away the tears coursing down her cheeks. "I can also tell you have fallen in love with Lord Worsley."

Marianne stood and went over to the windows overlooking the streets of the town. "It does not matter."

"Did he break your heart too?"

"No," she whispered. "But it is empty, and the things it needs to be filled with will never happen." She frowned at the carriage that pulled up outside at the entrance. Then shock bloomed through her as Mr. Thomas St. Ives descended, taking off his hat and crushing it in his hands.

"Lucy!"

She scrambled to her feet. "What is it?" she asked, rushing over.

When she saw him, she lurched back, gripping Marianne's shoulder. "Why is he here?"

She whirled at her sister's cry of alarm. The hope in Lucy's eyes strangled Marianne's breath.

"You would forgive him?" she asked her softly.

Lucy burst into tears, "I do not know. Because of him, our child is a bastard and might never find her place in this world! But Marianne I still love that wretched man with every beat of my heart."

Marianne hugged her sister to her. "She will. Her uncle is powerful and will do everything for her. I also suspect for Mr. St. Ives to be here it means he wants you and her. She will have you, her loving and devoted mother to guide her, and she will always have me."

Lucy nodded.

"Now compose yourself, wash your face and go down to him."

Her sister laughed and walked away. She gripped the knob and opened the door.

"Lucy?"

She glanced over her shoulder at Marianne. "Yes?"

"Let him grovel!"

Her sister's eyes widened and then she nodded, before closing the door and hurrying down the stairs. Marianne exhaled a sharp breath, and her wretched curiosity urged her to follow her sister and eavesdrop. She giggled and tossing her head she hurriedly shed her nightgown. She picked a light blue day dress with a tight waist and high lace collar. She hurried down the stairs to see the drawing-room door ajar, and two of Lucy's maids hovering close by. When they saw Marianne they scampered away, and she shamelessly went closer.

Mr. St. Ives was on his knees, peering up at Lucy, who seemed indifferent to his pleas.

"My sweet Lucy, I beg you, please put me out of my misery and consent to be my wife."

"Why should I?" she said with a haughty lift of her chin. "I am now a woman of independent means. I have this charming home and my own money. I also have a bevy of *beaux* demanding dances from me every night at the assembly rooms. I do not need you, Thomas!"

His face crumpled, and he staggered to his feet, and from where she stood, Marianne could see the agony on his face.

"You don't need me," he said softly. "and I am glad for it. But I fervently hope you could forgive me and learn to want me again as desperately as I want you, Lucy."

Her sister stared at him, and her lips wobbled, but to Marianne's shock she simply said, "I shall think about it, now if you will excuse me, I have to call upon my dear friend."

"I am staying at The White Hart hotel," he said, "Will you permit me to call upon you tomorrow?"

Marianne walked away, missing her sister's reply. A burst of pride filled her chest, knowing that everything would be quite well with her sister. The relief of it almost dragged Marianne to her knees, and deep down, a part of her knew that somehow Michael had something to do with Thomas's presence.

A few days later, Marianne departed Bath, leaving Lucy to run her tangled web around Thomas. Each day he visited, publicly courting her, and Lucy would remain aloof but then scream her happiness when he left. Marianne did not want to remain in Bath, for she missed her parents and her sisters. Lucy had wanted to settle five hundred pounds on Marianne, and she had informed her she would think about it.

As the private coach Lucy had hired to transport her rumbled over the rocky country road, Marianne turned her thoughts to her future. Settling down in Biddleton seemed impossible after only seeing a little of the world. Perhaps she could take the money Lucy offered, and her younger sister, Ruth, who was one and twenty, and perhaps hire a lady companion, then take a trip to Italy. She had no idea if the money would stretch that far, but it was a beautiful dream, one that would take her far away from Michael. She did not think she could bear to see him for many years to come.

There they could explore the ruins; maybe eventually the hollowness in her heart would be filled, and life would once again seem bright with endless adventures and possibilities. She let out a sigh of relief as her home came into view. Marianne had been traveling for several days, staying in respectable inns each night, and then leaving early the very next day to continue her journey home. Seeing that large cottage and inhaling the scent of a freshly baked cake, a sense of peace filled her chest.

The steps of the coach were knocked down, and she got off the carriage. The curtain in the parlor shifted, and a face peeked out the window.

"Marianne is home," Sarah cried.

The coachman set down her valises, and she located some coins which were hidden in a reticule deep within her hatbox and tipped him generously. He smiled, hopped onto his seat, and urged his horse away. When she turned around, her papa was there, coming down those small steps.

The wide smile which had curved his lips faded as he stared into her face. He flinched, and pain darkened his eyes. Marianne's heart broke into smaller pieces. He knew! She did not know what he saw in her face, but he knew. Emotions rose to choke her, and her lips trembled. She was mortified to feel the tears spilling over. Bracing for his anger…or worse his disappointment she closed her eyes on a choked gasp.

"Marianne."

She opened her eyes at that soft entreaty. Her papa stood with his arms wide open. Dropping her hatbox on the ground, she hurled into his arms, sobbing her heart out against his chest.

"I BEG YOUR PARDON?" The Earl of Kenwood said, his eyes darkening with shock and anger. "Your brother is breaking the engagement?"

"Yes," Michael smoothly replied, wondering if he

should point out to the man that his daughter, the very one they were discussing, was hiding behind the peach-colored drapes and listening to their conversation. That bit of naughty spirit amused him. Now he understood the ruinous manner in which the girl had acted. She was both willful and impetuous.

The earl's dark slashing brows lowered, and he narrowed his brown eyes threateningly. "I'll not allow it! It has already been announced! How dare you, Worsley? I'll sue your brother for breach of promise and—"

"I know about Lady Sarah's unfortunate little accident," he said softly. Michael had ruthlessly searched for any secrets the man might have, hoping for any leverage to ensure he came out the winner in this negotiation. Once again, he saw Marianne's disappointed green eyes, and he scowled.

"She was caught kissing your solicitor. A very ambitious man with dreams of holding a seat in parliament. Not the worst suitor she could have found. I even heard say that she is deeply in love with the young man, and that he sought her hand in marriage but you do not approve of the match."

The earl's cheeks went ruddy. "That was weeks' ago, only a kiss, and I fired him!"

"Nevertheless…I must insist the contract be canceled because you cannot expect my brother to marry a girl who is in love with another man."

"No, I'll not—"

The curtains were parted with such vigor they were nearly torn from their hooks, and a very beautiful young lady who could not be a day over seventeen rushed out from behind them, her hands clasped to her cheeks in a dramatic fashion.

"Papa! Surely you know Neil owns my heart! I shall die

and be prostrate with grief if you do not allow me to marry him." Her lips wobbled, and tears pooled into wide, big, beautiful golden-brown eyes.

With a groan, the earl stood. "Sarah! What did I tell you about hiding—"

"Papa!" she cried, stomping her feet. "I shall run away with him, I shall if you do not consent! I do not want to marry that odious Thomas St. Ives. Surely you must see that. Neil—."

"Mr. Stanton!" her father roared. "He is Mr. Stanton to you."

The girl did not even flinch at her father's anger, and Michael realized then how much the man had spoilt her. He came to his feet, amused by it all.

"Mr. Stanton," she said, "did not seek to kiss me or do anything wrong. He has always been scrupulously respectful. I heard you coming, Papa, and threw myself in his arms. Of course, he was helpless after that to resist my charms," she said with a pretty blush.

Good God.

Her father stared at her as if she had gone mad, and Michael swore he saw the formation of a few gray hairs at the earl's temple right before his very eyes! Imagine that.

"I believe I shall take my leave," he said smoothly.

"By God, Worsley, you will not leave!" the earl snapped, and in his eyes, Michael saw desperation.

It was that look and the image of Marianne's censure which gave him pause. "To atone for my brother's change of mind which I acknowledge is ungentlemanly conduct, I will settle a sum of twenty-five thousand pounds on your daughter." He would never mention he knew of the earl's impoverished state, and that was the reason the man had been so eager for an alliance with his family.

"Thirty-five thousand pounds!" the Earl countered.

A drop in the bucket of Michael's wealth. He cocked his head, thinking of the debts he had discovered the man owed. That amount should see him above water. "Done."

Relief rushed from the earl, and he gave him a considering glance. "Why did you do this, Worsley? You have the upper hand because of my daughter's ridiculous behavior. Thirty-five thousand pounds is no small matter."

"Papa!"

They ignored her.

Michael shrugged. "It is what Miss Ashbrook would want."

The bold chit stepped forward. "I also demand at least ten thousand pounds for my dowry. I am certain Miss Ashbrook would want that as well considering the damage your brother will do to my reputation once it is learned the engagement is no more!"

"I will allow you, Lady Sarah, the latitude of calling off the engagement for, of course, marrying a man you love, a rising star in politics who will have my support."

Interest lit in her eyes, and her father choked when she held out a hand for a shake.

"Very well, I shall count on your support for Neil…Mr. Stanton, in addition to the funds for my dowry. Imagine how distressed Miss Ashbrook would be if she learned otherwise."

Amusement curled through him. He shook her hand. "Done."

She clapped her hands in glee, and the stunned Lord Kenwood could only stare at him.

"Who is this Miss Ashbrook, if I may ask?"

"My reason for everything I've learned." Then he walked away, hoping she would take a chance on his love.

CHAPTER 18

A wonderful morning breeze wafted from the windows of the church. The large oak door groaned open, and a few people shifted to see the identity of the late arrival. The scandal of appearing tardily would be tittered about for all of this week until next week's service's latecomer took the honor. The people of Biddleton truly had little to amuse their imaginings or to keep their tongues occupied. Marianne did not move, folding her gloved hands in her lap and staring straight at her father. Curiosity bit at her, but of all places, this must be where she set an example for her sisters. Of course, Ruth, Sarah, and Maggie shamelessly turned in their seats.

"Our Lord is forgiving and merciful, for He loves us more than anything our humble minds and thoughts can ever imagine. Love is kind, and love forgives even the most egregious of sins because that is what our Lord commands through example—"

A ripple of murmurs in the congregation disturbed her father's sermon, and he faltered briefly. Marianne frowned and tried to ignore whatever had caused the commotion.

She sat on the fourth bench in the pews, after arriving at church this Sunday morning a few minutes late. Of course, a few of her father's parishioners had thought it necessary to whisper that the vicar's own daughter had shown up late. She had hardly cared, the ache in her heart had not eased. In truth, it had multiplied dreadfully with each day that passed.

Her dear papa had not pried; in his warm embrace, she only found love and forgiveness. Even though a part of her feared it might be because he did not know the full truth of her misbehaving heart. But that very first night she had returned home, he had whispered,

"*Though I see the pain in your eyes…I do not see regret or shame, and for that I am grateful.*"

"How handsome he is!" Sarah gasped.

"Do you see the carriage in which he came! It is pulled by a matched team of four, and his clothes; he is wealthy too." That loud whisper came from a few seats behind her.

Ruth's eyes widened. "I wonder who he is?"

"I don't care," Maggie said with a cheeky grin. "Nothing exciting happens in Biddleton."

Marianne rolled her eyes. "The arrival of a man can hardly be seen as an event to gossip about."

"Oh, Marianne, surely when you see him, you shouldn't think so. Why he is even more handsome than Squire Nelson and he is very fine indeed," Maggie said with a wink.

With annoying curiosity, Marianne turned around and immediately his gaze found hers. She drew in a shocked breath and whipped her head forward. "Good heavens!"

"I told you so," Maggie said, and then her eyes widened. "Marianne…you are flushed. Are you well?"

She froze, unable to explain the tangle of emotions she felt about. "I…What is he doing here?" she whispered.

Ruth covered Marianne's hand that gripped the edge of the bench with her own. "Is he the reason you returned from London so altered?"

She glanced at her sister.

"Do you believe we have not noticed you are not your usual self?"

Their father cleared his throat and frowned most severely at his congregation. The murmurs died then, and the next half hour passed for Marianne in an agonized blur. Unable to bear the mess of hope and hurt anymore, she launched to her feet and hurried away. His gaze followed her as she rushed outside, and it took an enormous will to not look back at him. She hurried home, grateful for the closeness of their cottage to the church. Marianne went to her room and tugged the bonnet from her head.

She closed her eyes and tried to think. Michael had followed her. *Why?* Surely it could not be to convince her to return to his home to be Lizzie's governess. Dear God, Lizzie! Marianne gasped. What if something had happened to her niece? She scrambled down the stairs, all anxiety at facing him melting away.

She heard voices coming from the parlor, and the sensual, familiar tones dragged her feet there. The viscount was seated with a cup of tea in his hand, her mother and father were already present, and so were her sisters who stared at him as if he were an exotic creature.

"So your brother is marrying our Lucy?" her mother asked faintly.

Marianne's heart jolted.

"Yes, I got the letter from him only a few days ago that she has consented to marry him. They will be taking their child…Lizzie on an extended vacation with them to a lovely country house in Cornwall. As my brother tells it, they will stay away from town society for a couple of years while they meet their country neighbors and enjoy that society. And when they are ready to announce their daughter, they will venture into town."

She must have made some sound, for she became the center of everyone's attention. When he saw her, he breathed deeply, his hungry stare caressing over her. She blushed and her father's eyes sharpened.

Michael stood. "Miss Ashbrook, how lovely to see you again."

Her father too stood. "I am astonished to learn that Lizzie has been with her uncle, Lord Worsley, all this time…and not in the orphanage you mentioned, Marianne."

There was a slight admonishment in his voice.

"And I am very glad she had the courage to defy your orders, Sir," Michael said firmly. "Or I might have never known my niece."

Her father's face softened. "I daresay a part of me knew that Marianne would defy my orders. That is why I allowed her to convince me that she would take the child. I could see the fire of rebellion in her eyes and her determination and I was glad for it. Forgive me, my child, for placing that burden on you."

She smiled at her papa and nodded, a most wonderful feeling swelling in heart. And because she could not keep the hope silent anymore, she looked at Michacl.

"Is that the only reason you came?"

"Marianne!" her mother said, leaping to her feet, "Forgive our daughter's rudeness, my lord."

But neither paid Mama any attention. The viscount was gazing at her as though she were some kind of miracle.

"I love you," he said. "And I was hoping you might do me the honor of marrying me."

Marianne almost fainted. That was the very last thing she had expected him to say and certainly not the first.

Her father's gaze moved from her to the viscount. And from the corner of her eyes she could see the delight on her sisters' faces.

"You love me?" she parroted, her heart crashing inside her chest; she felt faint.

"Yes."

"And you want to marry me?" she squawked.

Tender amusement shifted in his gaze. "Ah…there goes that mouse again."

"Now is not the time to jest," she cried, so many emotions assailing her. Tears formed in her eyes and she fought to contain them. "You…you are a viscount, one who owns a gambling den and I am only the daughter of a country vicar!"

It felt so impossible but so right.

"Society might say that I am a wicked man, and a rake of the first order as you so charmingly put it. Yet, I believe with all my heart, only God could have understood the constant loneliness that I felt in my heart and then contrived to place you in my path."

She stared at him in wordless wonder.

Her mother placed her knitting needles on the walnut table, stood, and held out her hand to her husband. Papa took her hand, and to Marianne's shock, they departed the parlor with her sisters, leaving her alone with the viscount. She stared at their retreating backs, almost scared to face him. A wobbly smile curved her lips when they left the door a little ajar. Marianne could not shift her regard back to Michael. She was petrified for some reason. "Perhaps this *is* a dream," she murmured.

"Look at me."

A soft gasp escaped her at the feel of his warm breath on her ear. He was too close. Surely, he could see the door stood open. "Michael—"

"Look at me," he said, his voice tender and resonating with an affection that brought a lump to her throat.

She turned slowly and faced him.

"Why did you run from me?"

"I was afraid," she said hoarsely.

He touched her chin ever so lightly with his thumb. "If you had only stayed…there wouldn't have been any doubts in your mind that I belong only to you."

A trembling sigh fell from her lips. "It took you three weeks to find me." *And all that time…I died.*

"It was most inconsiderate of me," he said tenderly. "I am so damn sorry." He cupped her cheek, and she leaned into his palm. "I had to fix things first…How could I come to you when your heart was still broken from your sister's pain."

The purest of joy blossomed through her. "You are responsible for Thomas coming to Lucy?"

"He only needed a nudge."

"But the scandal!"

"I took care of it," he said gently. "And I daresay that his ex-fiancée might be more thrilled than Thomas and Lucy. And I also ensured that the young miss is safely away with her sisters and that her uncle cannot steal her fortune. I hope you approve."

"Oh, Michael." She flung herself into his arms and hugged him.

"Though I am very glad you are in my arms," he said, his heart pounding where her ear rested against his chest. "Please relieve my fear and tell me if you will consent to be my wife."

She leaned back a bit and stared at him. "Your wife."

He cupped her cheeks tenderly. "My wife…my friend, my lover, my partner in misadventures. Before you came into my life, nothing seemed to matter anymore. I had wealth, ladies throwing themselves at my feet and in my bed—"

She punched him lightly in the stomach and an unrepentant grin crossed his lips.

"And I have been declining all of them, my love. You were the first woman I kissed, made love with in over a year. No-one enticed me…nothing appealed, and then you came into my life…and you brought me in from the cold, lonely place I had not realized I lived in."

"I love you," she said on a choked cry, tears streaming down her face. "I love you with my entire heart and yes, I will marry you!"

He pressed a kiss to her lips, and murmured against them, "I thank you for that honor and I shall endeavor to never make you regret it."

A throat cleared and Marianne giggled against his lips. "My papa was eavesdropping." Then she blushed fiercely praying he had not overheard that 'make love' bit.

"I daresay I consent to this union," her father's voice said from outside the door. "But until that time, I trust, young man, you will remove your lips from my daughter."

Marianne dissolved into fits of giggles while Michael smiled at her with tender amusement.

"That I can do, Sir. I do have a special license—"

"No!" she gasped. "I want a grand wedding. And then a honeymoon to Italy and Versailles!"

"Then you shall have it! However, I insist your father conducts the wedding service."

"And my sisters can be bridesmaids?"

"But, of course. Will a week be long enough? If

everyone were to travel to London tomorrow, I can make all the arrangements."

And before she could move again, he took her in his arms once again and simply held her close to him.

"I love you," she whispered fiercely. "And I too will endeavor to make you very happy. Michael."

THANK you for reading **Sins of Viscount Worsley**!

I hope you enjoyed the journey to happy ever after for Marianne & Worsley. **REVIEWS ARE GOLD TO AUTHORS,** for they are a very important part of reaching readers, and I do hope you will consider leaving an honest review on Amazon adding to my rainbow. It does not have to be lengthy, a simple sentence or two will do. Just know that I will appreciate your efforts sincerely.

ACKNOWLEDGMENTS

I thank God every day for my family, friends, and writing. A special thank you to my husband. I love you so hard! You encourage me to dream and are always steadfast in your incredible support. You read all my drafts, offer such fantastic insight and encouragement. Thank you for designing my fabulous cover! Thank you for reminding me I am a warrior when I wanted to give up on so many things.

Thank you, Giselle Marks for being so wonderful and supportive always. You are a great critique partner and friend.

Readers, thank you for giving me a chance and reading my book! I hope you enjoyed and would consider leaving a review. Thank you!

ABOUT STACY

USA Today Bestselling author Stacy Reid writes sensual Historical and Paranormal Romances and is the published author of over twenty books. Her debut novella The Duke's Shotgun Wedding was a 2015 HOLT Award of Merit recipient in the Romance Novella category, and her bestselling Wedded by Scandal series is recommended as Top picks at Night Owl Reviews, Fresh Fiction Reviews, and The Romance Reviews.

Stacy lives a lot in the worlds she creates and actively speaks to her characters (aloud). She has a warrior way "Never give up on dreams!" When she's not writing, Stacy spends a copious amount of time binge-watching series like The Walking Dead, Altered Carbon, Rise of the Phoenixes, Ten Miles of Peach Blosson, and playing video games with her love. She also has a weakness for ice cream and will have it as her main course.

Stacy is represented by Jill Marsal at Marsal Lyon Literary Agency.

She is always happy to hear from readers and would love to connect with you via my Website, Facebook, and Twitter. To be the first to hear about her new releases, get cover reveals, and excerpts you won't find anywhere else, sign up for her newsletter, or join her over at Historical Hellions, her fan group!

BB Follow me on BookBub

Printed by Amazon Italia Logistica S.r.l.
Torrazza Piemonte (TO), Italy

16716817R00116